WITHDRAWN

Move!

Move!

by JOEL LIEBER

DAVID McKAY COMPANY, INC.

New York

MOVE!

Library of Congress Catalog Card Number: 68-19924

MANUFACTURED IN THE UNITED STATES OF AMERICA

VAN REES PRESS • NEW YORK

To Sylvia

Move!

ONE

An eruption of hoofbeats shattered the quiet of the late afternoon. The young man, preoccupied and daydreaming, cursed. He called to his flock: "Murphy, Sugar, Gregory, Banjo, Omar, Hans. C'mon. C'mere."

Whistling and clapping his hands, and afraid the rider might trample one of them, he got five, but Omar, the Saluki, broke for the horse, possibly mistaking the animal for an Arabian gazelle.

The rider reined up, his mount dancing nervously to the right. Omar's nose was wrinkled, his teeth threatening the rider's boots. "Get 'im on the leash, Jaffe. Get 'im on the leash," he yelled.

When the dog was leashed, he bawled, "Jaffe, goddamit man, how long are you going to flaunt the authority of the law? It's gotta stop."

"There's nobody around, not a soul. They weren't bothering anyone."

It was true. In the sheltered wood where he walked the dogs, the park was deserted.

"Whaddya call *that?*" the rider demanded, pointing at Omar, whose lips were drawn back and trembling.

"You scared him, Hobbs. It's your fault, not mine. You come charging down here like a Canadian Mountie or something."

"I got my orders. Those dogs gotta be on the leash."

"Not today, Hobbs. Do me a favor, not today. It's been a bad day. Can't we do this business some other time?"

From four feet above him, the policeman glowered down at Jaffe. Steam rose from the horse's flanks. The policeman drew himself up in a creaking of leather and set one arm on his hip. Nature had given him the squarest of jaws and he knew how to make the most of it. "I've been patient with you, Jaffe. Really patient."

It was a game they had been through twenty times, back and forth, Hobbs taking the pompous and official part: get them on the leash Jaffe; but they need the exercise Hobbs; it's the law Jaffe; but it's my livelihood Hobbs; I've got my orders Jaffe; but I've got to make a buck Hobbs; people complain Jaffe; what people Hobbs; they call the precinct Jaffe; only the queers are afraid of the dogs; I don't like this any more than you do; then look for the perverts and leave us alone Hobbs.

The horse was new. Hobbs used to be on the Tactical Force and had been assigned to the queer detail in the park. But the queers were foxy and hard to find, especially the ones who exposed themselves to mothers strolling with baby carriages. Once Hobbs popped out from behind a tree in street clothes, angered at not having caught a

2

single deviate all day, and proceeded to give Jaffe hell for letting his dogs off the leash. Six months ago he had the motor scooter detail, but a pervert could hear the thing a mile off and now Hobbs, the frustrated queer-chaser, went after them on a great brown charger.

He leaned down in the saddle, a finger wagging at Jaffe, "You've got a right to make a living, but at the same time you've got to stay within the law."

Jaffe sniffed. For a moment he thought he smelled liquor on his breath. Hobbs drew back when he saw the dog-walker's nostrils quiver. The horse shook his head, and for a second it occurred to Jaffe that the alcohol was on the horse's breath, too. Was it possible?

"You take advantage of me, Jaffe. You don't take me seriously."

"I get away with murder," Jaffe added, anticipating the next rebuke.

"You've got this coming, Jaffe. You keep disregarding one law over and over, and one thing leads to the next, and pretty soon you've got a complete breakdown of law and order."

"Hobbs, you know damn well that these dogs keep the perverts away. You told me yourself that you never see them up here where I take the dogs. They're afraid of them."

"Fuck the perverts," snapped Hobbs.

"Sir?"

"I'm telling you to leave the perverts to me. They're my work. I'm telling you about law and order."

Jaffee, bored with the conversation, glanced over at Banjo, the English bull. He was working over the base of

3

a tree. Jaffe tallied it up in his head: that was the last one. Now he could take them back and get home to see if they called.

"I'm going home, Hobbs."

"Not so fast," the policeman said.

Jaffe looked up and was startled to see Hobbs writing on a sheath of tickets.

"Hobbs, you can't be serious."

"It's the law. You're still young, Jaffe. You gotta learn about the law. You gotta have respect for it. That's the conclusion I've come to."

"Hobbs. Hobbsie *baby*."

"One of those dogs'll bite someone one day and then you'll be in real trouble."

"But I'm covered. All the dogs I walk are insured."

"I'm doing this for your own good. One day you'll thank me," he said, handing him the ticket.

"Son of a bitch," Jaffe muttered.

"WHAT? What was that?"

"I said I've got an itch," Jaffe lied, remembering to reach down and scratch his knee.

He delivered the bulldog to Mrs. Ribble, the Airedale to the Burkes, the Saluki to the Simons, and, before returning Hans, the Katzes' shepherd, he detoured back to see if the truck was on his street.

It wasn't.

He dropped off Hans and returned home with his own dog, Murphy, a two-hundred pound Saint Bernard bitch.

It was developing into an inauspicious day for Jaffe—cold, autumnal, windy, and now a ticket. Nothing was

4

going right and he had begun to feel the strain of it in his stomach. Climbing the steps of his brownstone, Murphy glanced up at him, as if she had received his distress signals along the leash. Her big, wet, drooping eyes offered their assistance.

The living room was a mess of boxes. They were piled up all in a rough sort of grouping, twenty-three boxes collected from groceries, supermarkets and liquor stores over the past two weeks, waiting to be moved out. His wife Dolly sat on the piano bench, her back leaning against the piano and her feet up on a box out of which a frying pan arm protruded. She was smoking and appeared perfectly calm. "I was just thinking," she said as he came in, as if picking up the thread of a conversation, "do you know how much he made last year?"

"Who?"

"Dr. Picker."

Jaffe said nothing.

"Sixty . . . seven . . . thousand . . . dollars." The way she drew out each word gave it the ring of sixty-seven million.

"So?"

"*So?*" she repeated, startled, as though no sane person could miss the implication.

"Forget about Picker for a minute," Jaffe said, unleashing Murphy. "They call while I was out?"

"Who?"

"Who do you think?"

"Oh. No. Nobody called."

It was after five o'clock and the movers were supposed to have come at noon. He had begun to find the delay intolerable, maddening, although he didn't precisely know why.

He went to the phone and dialed their office. The call he had made earlier, at three o'clock, connected him with a bored, flighty-sounding girl who assured him that they would be at his house any minute. "Momentarily," she had said, displaying the word like it was the biggest one she knew. But at four, when he called again, she wasn't there and an answering service picked up the message. Even the answering service woman seemed surprised that no one was at the office.

"Movers," the flighty girl now answered.

"It's me again. Hiram Jaffe. Have you heard anything? They still haven't come."

"Oh, it's you," she said. "Well, there's bound to be some delay."

"What does that mean—*bound* to be some delay? What does that mean?"

"They got this *m'shuga* super on their first job and he delayed them. They couldn't get started on time. I spoke to Charley at three-thirty, and he told me he was making progress. He said he'd have the boss call you personally."

"Nobody called, neither personally nor impersonally."

"I'm very surprised," she said indifferently.

"So where do we stand? When should I expect them?"

"Well," said the girl, "if I were you, I'd stand by the old phonereeno. And as soon as—." He strained to catch some clues through the earpiece. If he could only see her eyes. He seemed to feel, through the miles of telephone wire, that she was stalling him. The truck had four flats. One of the movers had an appendicitis attack. Why

6

couldn't she just tell him the truth? He sensed that she knew more than she was telling him. What instructions had they given her about him?

"All right," he said, "but tell them we'd really like to get going. This is throwing everything way off."

"What's way off? It's only a couple of hours."

"Five hours is more than a couple," Jaffe said, working to keep his voice from getting away. In the back of his mind was the thought that if he really got mad at the girl they'd call the whole deal off and just not show up at all.

"What're you, Mr. Jaffe—religious? You don't work on Friday nights? If that's your problem, why didn't you make an appointment for another day?"

"It has nothing to do with religion. If you must know, it happens I'm a Zoroastrian. I believe the first man and woman grew from rhubarb stalks."

"I'll call you as soon as I hear anything," she said dryly.

Jaffe glanced at his wife. She was still smoking and had the sparkle of sixty-seven thousand dollars in her eyes. It was funny about Dolly: just lately she had the sexual history of a thousand New Yorkers at her fingertips. Six months ago she had gone to work for this man Picker, a psychiatrist, answering his phone, making appointments and typing his dictated case notes from a machine that plugged into her ear. She came home nights with incredible stories of sickness and depravity. Before Jaffe went to pick up his afternoon dogs, Dolly had been telling him about a new patient who had started the day before, a skinny man who had gone on a macrobiotic diet, starving himself and doing Yoga exercises so that he could perform

7

a strange rite on himself. "What do you mean, *strange rite?*" he had asked her. 'Auto-fellatio," Dolly replied. "I never heard of that," he told her. "Neither did I. But that's what Dr. Picker called it on dictation." "By Christ," Jaffe said, "the man's got a talent. He ought to go on the Ed Sullivan show with a trick like that."

Dolly hadn't found his suggestion funny—she took her work seriously—and had rounded out the story: "Wait, there's worse." Jaffe's eyes had widened, waiting for the next detail. Dolly's job was like having a daily, serialized version of the unpublished Krafft-Ebing papers. "He's married and his wife knows about it." Jaffe protested. "You made that up, Dolly." "No, I swear. I took it off the tape that way." "Then it's Dr. Picker. He sits in there all day making these goddam stories up." She became indignant. "He does not. Besides, I saw the man." Jaffe was interested in this. "What does he look like?" His wife shrugged. "Kind of average."

Jaffe glanced out the window. The last of the men working on the new building across the street were leaving. Ebbing sunlight from over the Jersey Palisades sent the shadows of the girders tumbling in confusion. They were a rough bunch, and any one of them was capable of raping Dolly if he could get away undetected, Jaffe thought. Each morning, when she came out of the building, they set on her with a chorus of obscenities, laying aside their jackhammers and paying their own kind of homage to the fresh and swinging, high-heeled way that Dolly had of bouncing out into a new day. "Hey baby, d'ja ever do it in the cab of a derrick?" "Hey baby, betcha I'm better'n

8

the college guys." It angered Jaffe that they said those things to Dolly, that she had to be subjected to them. Every day she ran the gantlet of their jibes, and it had occurred to Jaffe that his wife didn't seem a whit as bothered by them as he did. He had to concede privately that she might even enjoy the morning ritual.

He had even asked Hobbs whether anything could be done about the vile way they talked to his wife, a charge of public nuisance or some such thing. Jaffe had a vision of bringing them up before the judge, fingering the worst violators, and that after the judge fined them twenty-five dollars for disturbing the peace, their pals would lay for him at night, a pair of laborers with hands like sledge-hammers who would break up his guts and close his eyes. "Next time ya keep ya mouth shut," one would say, driving a knee into Jaffe's groin. Nor would Murphy's great bulk protect him. She was big and powerful, but a terrible coward; only yesterday it had taken Jaffe five minutes to calm her when an old lady's miniature Schnauzer snarled at her in the drug store. After his beating, however, it was probable that Murphy would lick his wounds. Hobbs had advised Jaffe not to pay attention to the workers, that they were really harmless and were all good family men at heart.

Jaffe watched as a big man in a plaid shirt and orange boots threw a lunchbox into the back seat of a new Chevrolet. A hefty woman, mother of the man's five tough kids, had packed the lunchbox for him, and soon he would be at home where he would have five bottles of beer to wash down a great dish of stew and potatoes. In between beers, Jaffe imagined, he would whack his kids around

9

for making too much noise. The next day his wife would wash his overalls with something she had seen a woman wash overalls with on a television commercial, while her husband resumed his station across the street, shouting obscenities at Dolly.

But right there, Jaffe considered, right there the big man was in for a surprise. No more Dolly. We'll be moved out. And we'll be able to sleep in the morning, too, without the unremitting pounding and grinding that starts up at seven o'clock. In certain respects, that was an even stronger motive for moving than the foul-mouthed laborers. Jaffe abhorred waking up with his heart racing to an eruption of whines, crashes, and air-hammer blasts. Curiously enough, Dolly slept right through the racket. She didn't have to get up till eight o'clock, and by that time Jaffe was dressed, breakfasted, and ready to pick up his customers' dogs for the morning walk. He had gone so far as to call a city office to check on the legality of starting the work at seven, and was assured that seven, by city ordinance, was the proper starting hour. Some people in the brownstone next door, and from nearby brownstones, had got together a petition to protest the early morning noise, but Jaffe felt they were being stupid. "It's not going to do any good," he told Dolly. "I'm not going to get emotionally involved in this. I'm no activist. My energies are otherwise directed." She answered, "You mean inwardly, right?"

That part would also change after they moved. No more people banging on their door and waving petitions for him to sign, no more being made to feel guilty for not signing them. His doorman would keep out all petitioners.

Dolly, although she hadn't been particularly disturbed either by the builders, the building noises, or the petitioners, admitted to distress over the way their dreams were being interrupted by the early morning noise. She had read an article in one of Dr. Picker's journals that convinced her they had to move. The psychiatrist reported a high incidence of frustration neurosis produced by the effect of low-flying airplanes that came in for pre-dawn landings, disrupting the dreams of residents in houses along the approach. "It's the same thing with the noise across the street," she told her husband. "Dreams have a continuity and they have to be completed. Otherwise, it's very unhealthy for you."

As though the apartment had ever been quiet in the first place. Jaffe knew all the romantic stories about the greatness of brownstones: you move into a brownstone and it's not like one of those new high-risers; in a brownstone you've got something substantial; it's quiet—the walls, thick; you can't hear a thing from the next apartment. Bullshit! Who on earth started stories like that? Jaffe felt it must be the same people who rap on the fenders of thirty-year-old cars and tell you about the solid steel and how the cars nowadays are made out of junky tin stuff. The couple above them had a baby two months old and the kid had a pair of lungs that could penetrate anything, brownstone walls and solid steel fenders put together. And when his mother got up in the middle of the night to feed the kid, the floors above would positively creak as she walked him up and down. Even the funny, soothing, crooning song she used on him would somehow filter down to Jaffe. One night he swore he could hear the

11

actual sucking noise that the baby was making at the breast. Brownstones my ass.

It was not simply the physical change of circumstances that inspired the move. From Jaffe's point of view, there were other considerations. For one thing, the new address would halt the flow of Jewish mail. He had already made it clear to the post office people, that he considered the solicitations an act of criminal intrusion. They gave him a form to fill out but told him that it would only stop the third- and fourth-class transfers. There was, he suspected, a good chance that the solicited groups had paid off the postal workers, possibly even offering scholarships to the children of cooperative post office men. He believed it began with the subscription to a Jewish intellectual magazine his parents had given him for his birthday. Soon afterward, the material came pouring into his mailbox and he had no choice but to assume that the mailing lists were being sold and resold all over the world. Demands for money poured in from the Jewish philanthropic societies, for the support of a Jewish school in Jerusalem that aided orphaned, left-handed Moroccan girls; for a Jewish old-age home in Youngstown, Ohio; for sending *matzoh* to Russia, for the upkeep of a cemetery on Long Island. It was as though they were trying to take advantage of Jaffe, having discovered that the building going up across the street was to contain a synagogue on the ground floor (right hand entrance). Of course, the latter was only a rumor, but he didn't dare to check it, because if it turned out to be true, then anything at all could happen to him. He didn't want to think about the implications: he had enough reason for moving without that.

12

A ringing phone brought him out of his reverie.

He grabbed it up. The movers? "Yes?"

"Telephone company, Mr. Jaffe. Just want to tell you that we're working on your request to keep your present line open. It's after five, and Friday as well, but your request has reached dispatch control and it's being handled right now. I can't tell you for certain that it'll work out but I want to assure you we're trying our best down here to accommodate you."

"God bless you," Jaffe said. "That's the first good news I've had today."

"It's not easy. In an emergency like this, when a customer needs his phone open for calls after he already requested that service be stopped on Friday at five—well, we literally spare nothing to hold up the shut-off order."

"That's really swell," said Jaffe, experiencing a sudden warm feeling for the gang down at the phone company.

"We got a dozen people working on it."

"A dozen? Is that necessary?"

"Believe me, it's not easy to stop a shut-off order once it's been routed. You got to catch it at the right spot."

"I didn't realize it was so complicated. If I did, I mean—"

"You still want the service on, don't you?"

"Yes, yes. Definitely. I'm expecting some important calls here."

"Reason I ask is one man already got himself tangled up in the wiring system while he was on the assignment. Another man went in after him, an old-timer who really knows the wires. They got an emergency crew down there."

"But I thought it was all done with machines. I didn't know you had to send men down there. I didn't think it worked that way."

"The guy's covered. We got a good medical plan. Last I heard his wife is standing by. She's keeping a vigil."

"Oh my God."

"It's touch and go."

"I . . . I feel so *responsible*. I mean, if I'd known what was involved . . ."

"He may not make it. He's been down there an awful long time, that's all *I* know."

"But isn't there anything I can do to help? What if I cancelled the request? Would that do any good?"

"You mean cancel the request that requested we rescind the shut-off request?"

"Yes, that's right."

"You dirty son of a bitch!"

Something made a snap in Jaffe's ear and then the dial-tone buzzed on.

At the far end of the one-room studio they were abandoning, Dolly was opening a can of dog food for Murphy. The odor from the punctured can drifted across the room to invade Jaffe's nose; it was the first time in a long time that the smell bothered him.

"I think I'll go over to the other place and see how the painter's doing. He should be ready to knock off. I guess I'll have to tell the new super that we'll be a little late moving in. I hope he won't mind."

"Who called?" Dolly asked.

That irritated Jaffe, the way Dolly did that.

"Did you hear what I said?" Jaffe asked his wife.

14

"Of course I heard. We're in the same room. But who was on the phone?"

"Then why can't you at least acknowledge that you heard, instead of changing the subject?"

"Hiram," Dolly asserted, as if she were saying, "For Christ's sake."

"While I'm out somebody from the phone company may call. Just tell him I'm not here, and don't get into any long discussions. They got some kind of a joker working there today."

"I've never heard of a joker at the phone company."

"Well, they got one there today. That, or they're less efficient than they let on."

"What do you mean?"

"Never mind. It's not important."

Dolly had been conducting her end of the conversation while scooping out the contents of the can. She set the bowl down and turned to face Jaffe.

"Hiram, do you know what I think?"

"What?"

"You're getting that funny sound around the edge of your voice again."

"I can't help it."

"Why? What's such a big deal?"

"It's the uncertainty. When are they going to come? Why can't they at least tell you?"

"So they'll come tomorrow," Dolly said. "Why is it so important? What difference does it make?"

"How do you know they'll come tomorrow? Or at all? They haven't said."

"Hiram, you're making a big thing out of nothing. Why

don't you go to the movies or something. Relax. I'll stay here."

"No. I want to be here when it happens."

"When *what* happens?"

Jaffe stood up and took hold of a rubber plant. "So long as I'm going over to see the painter, I might as well take a plant with me."

"Hiram, please calm down."

"Dolly, don't be commonplace."

"What do you mean?"

"In your language."

"HIRAM!" she yelled for effect, not knowing what else to say.

Jaffe went out with the plant, and Murphy flew through the door after him. He walked quickly in his silly gait, his feet turned in, as if he were an Australian tennis player trying to imitate Jackie Robinson. It was a hereditary trait, bowed legs, and he was certain he would pass it on to their child. Unborn and unconceived, his child was destined to have the Jaffe legs. Only Jaffe wouldn't drag him around to orthopedists the way his parents had done with him, shackling him with brace-like torture devices while he slept, in an effort to make his legs look like everyone else's. They were a sign that marked a man a Jaffe, a male-linked *xy*-thing in the chromosomes where no orthopedist could ever get his hands on it. Nor did Jaffe see it negatively. The day could come when some future Jaffe, doing important work, found himself pursued along the back streets of Tangiers. A gowned, dark-eyed man would hiss from a doorway, "I see by your gait that you are a Jaffe. We have been expecting you. In here, quickly."

16

A boat would leave in half an hour, and a man who knew the coastline perfectly would guide the Jaffe with the inturned step.

The building to which they were moving, for multiple and good reasons, was fifteen stories high and had an elevator and a doorman. It was three rooms, five blocks away, and would cost them thirty dollars more a month. Their new place, Jaffe liked to tell people, was on the penultimate floor.

In this door-manned tower of silence, he would be free from the roar of building noises, petitioners, and high school drop-outs-turned-foul-mouthed-laborers. Now that his income was secure, he could get on with the new play he had been writing. There was no reason to think of failure at thirty, not for a playwright, at least. Nor was he unknown and unproduced. Four years ago, the year he and Dolly were married, he had had two one-actors produced. *Easy on the Ketchup* and *The Butterfly King* only ran four weeks, but they got good reviews. In the second year of his marriage, he acquired both an agent and a two-thousand-dollar option from a Broadway producer for his play, *Sing Lulu a Lullaby*. It was a domestic comedy about a pregnant college girl home with her family during Christmas vacation. But disaster wrote the two-thousand-dollar check; it developed that the producer, in giving Jaffe the money, tied up the play for a year to other bidders. He did this because he was bringing out another play in a month with a similar basic situation and wanted to eliminate possible competition. That play, *The Love Game,* ran two and a half months. When the truth was known, Asch, Jaffe's agent, tried to console him by observing that it happened all the time: a tough break, yeah, but not so unusual. Asch claimed—and Jaffe didn't know whether to believe him—that the producer even apologized to him at a party and confided that Jaffe's was really the better play and that if he had the choice he would have preferred *Sing Lulu*.

Afterward, the incident settled inside Jaffe like glue, blocking the free flow of emotion and idea. He was choked with the futility of writing plays. He went into mental retreat, and through a connection of his brother Oscar—who thrived on contacts—he took a job writing brochures for an airline. But he quit after eight weeks, much to his brother's displeasure. "How does that make *me* look?" Jaffe's brother demanded.

A friend of Jaffe's then put him on to a Times Square bookdealer who paid five hundred dollars for original novels of pornographic sadism (deliberately aimed at an audience of sexual deviates). Jaffe did three, finding the first one amusing, the second boring, and the third disgusting. He went on to find another temporary market, free-lance greeting cards, and became a specialist in eight-line Mother's Day cards. Finally, he hit on the dog-walking scheme, a natural outgrowth of getting Murphy. He now cleared a steady fifty dollars a week walking the dogs, and it took no more than two hours a day of his time. Occasionally he picked up some extra money by feeding and walking a dog when the owners went away on a trip: $1.50 a feed-and-walk. Jaffe's latent businessman's genes, swarming someplace in the same confusion with the bowed-leg genes, had even brought him to place an ad in a sleazy men's magazine:

18

HOW TO MAKE $$$$$ IN YOUR SPARE TIME

Get up just one hour earlier
each day and add $50 a week
to your income. No capital
outlay.
How is it possible?
Just send one dollar to
P.O.B. 7535. New York 10025.

It had been only a hunch, but during the past year it had brought in seven hundred dollars, more than making up for box rental and the offset prospectus describing the fine points of developing a going dog-walking operation. There had been a dollar bill in the mail only yesterday.

Little of which, Alfred Spiegler, the brownstone's superintendent, knew anything about. Spiegler always wore an annoyed look when Jaffe returned to the building with Murphy and the newspaper around nine o'clock in the morning. Everyone was bustling off to the subway, and Spiegler personally resented the fact that a normal healthy person shouldn't be going downtown to put in a day's work. He lacked the imagination to consider Jaffe anything but a wastrel who lived off his wife—that pretty, friendly, young woman who went out to work every morning and gave him such a nice greeting. Once, when Spiegler asked Dolly what her husband did in the house all day, Dolly replied, "Oh, he's thinking." Spiegler believed the girl and pitied her for being married to a bum.

Still, for Jaffe, there had evolved a certain rhythm to those days in the brownstone, a settling in. The apartment was both defined and confined. But now his life was piled into those boxes and he once again became a victim

19

of his imagination. It was intimately connected with this move, that much he knew. Some big trouble, long overdue and until recently vague, was moving in on him just as he was moving out.

He opened the door and smiled at the painter atop the ladder. The painter didn't smile back.

A terror-struck woman jumped behind the ladder as Murphy thumped into the apartment. Jaffe leashed in the dog who, tongue out and rear end swishing to and fro, struggled to convey her good will.

"Almost finished for the day, Mr. Lopez?" Jaffe asked.

The painter scowled. "My wife," he said, introducing the portly little woman in distress behind the ladder.

"How do you do?" said Jaffe.

A sob burst from the woman. She pulled at her husband's paint-stained pants and squealed to him in trembling, excited Spanish.

Now what? Jaffe wondered. He surveyed the living room, where only one wall remained to be painted avocado, then glanced guiltily at the painter and his wife, as though he had intruded. It occurred to him that even though it was his apartment, perhaps he should have knocked before coming in.

"It needs much longer time," the painter said. "These colors," he gesticulated, wearing a pained, sour expression on his face. He shook his head. The painter's wife went right on tugging his pants.

Dolly had insisted on doing the apartment like a coloring book. Jaffe tended to agree that he didn't care for a sterile, all-white apartment, but he didn't anticipate that the new landlord wouldn't (*couldn't* was the word he used) provide a union painter for a big color job. Instead, Dolly got a cash settlement from the landlord and hired a painter through the recommendation of a local hardware store. "He needs the work," the hardware man said. "I think he's honest and he's got six kids."

Jaffe brought the plant into the bedroom which yesterday had been painted a deep Wedgwood blue. It was dry, and with the painter's rags gone, the room perfectly empty, the walls echoed each footstep. Murphy sneezed heavily. Jaffe opened a window and thought the painter stupid for leaving the window closed: the room smelled awful.

He ducked into the bathroom for a quick check. It was painted Kansas barn red, the four walls and ceiling. The sink looked like it had the measles. Jaffe wondered whether he should bring this sloppy sort of work to the painter's attention. But what if the man became angry, and quit, flicking his red paint brush all over the blue bedroom, perhaps, in his Puerto Rican anger, spattering Murphy's coat with avocado green? Better forget that, Jaffe decided.

Glancing into the kitchen, he found it still wet, shining alive under a brilliant coat of Mexican sun orange. Murphy sneezed again.

The painter and his wife were shouting at each other.

"Excuse me," said Jaffe, "does this have anything to do with me or is it strictly a domestic matter?"

Jaffe winced slightly as the painter put an oily hand over his wife's mouth, silencing her cries. "Yesterday, my Antonio in a fight," he said, and made a gouging motion in his stomach. "He hurt. In hospital. Now my Angel look

21

for boy who do this to his brother. He want to kill him. My wife say I come home stop him."

The woman poked her husband anxiously. He released his hold over her mouth.

"She no want Angel in trouble. One enough. I tell her, 'Rosa, I work. I can no stop and run away.'"

Could it be, Jaffe wondered, that this is just a ruse to knock off early? Or could it mean that the man was not terribly interested in the fate of his unmanageable sons and really preferred to let the community take care of them? Jaffe felt he didn't have enough information to go on, but he was also aware that if the second boy got his jugular severed trying to avenge his brother, he, Jaffe, would know the pain.

"Mr. Lopez, forget the fourth wall today. Do it tomorrow. Go find your son. Please don't use me as an excuse for not going."

The painter took a tentative step down the ladder. "But you no understand. I tell you I have other job begin tomorrow. When I finish?"

"What's more important? My avocado wall or your son's life? Just go. I don't want to have any responsibility —none, however indirect—for your Angel's life."

"I no understand what you say."

"Do you understand *go?*"

"Go? Leave?"

"Yes."

"I go."

The painter and his wife left without saying goodbye.

Jaffe put the brush in a turpentine bucket and then bent down to the can, fastening the lid on.

22

It occurred to him that when the movers finally brought over his boxes and piano and furniture, there would be all this paint stuff around, not to mention an unpainted wall. Obstacles were piling up like a barricade. But there's one I can remove, he decided. At the same time I can do the painter a good turn. Who knows? It could help turn matters for the better, assuming, as was his infantile want, that the forces operated in a certain balance. "Sit down, Murph old girl," he instructed the dog. "This won't take long." He removed the top from the can and pushed it all toward the white wall—paint bucket, ladder, and rags.

This move is going to work, he told himself, I hope, I hope, I hope. He began with big broad strokes from the top border, laying the paint on thick. When he felt a wet sprinkling across the top of his head, he touched his hair and found his hand moist with avocado. If I work fast, but not sloppily, I can get it finished in a half hour, and then get back to Dolly, where surely, as a result of my good actions, the movers will already be taking the things out. He jumped down from the ladder and tore off his clothes, everything, socks included. He put on the painter's gloves and sprang back up the ladder.

This was the way to get a job done. Insensibly, he sought to strike a bargain with some greater power: what'll you give me in exchange for painting this wall, in, say, thirty minutes flat? A play produced? Moved in by nine o'clock? Love for my Dolly? Yes, this is the way to get a job done. This is how the undaunted men of old would have tackled a problem, he thought, slapping on brush after brush. Droplets of green flew onto his shoulders and chest. A fury took hold of him as he worked. He considered the men of old: Avram, the monumentalist of Constantinople, begat Moshe who, like his father before him, was also a Constantinople monumentalist; Moshe begat Misha, who crossed the Black Sea to Odessa; Misha, who was a barber, lived to be 90 and begat Khazkel, who moved his family to Liedze, near Cracow, and was murdered in a pogrom, although not before he begat Yakov, who became a rabbi in Ptock, on the banks of the Vistula; and Yakov begat Zalman, baker of breads and cakes, who begat a tailor, Aaron, who fled a Cossack onslaught and settled in Gdansk, where he begat first two daughters and then Shaul, and then took a trip to New York. In New York, Shaul begat Oscar, now 39, and Hiram, 30, playwright, ex-pornographist, greeting-card writer, dogwalker, wall-painter.

Paint swamped the wall. Sickening fumes filled his nose. Naked on the ladder, Jaffe had a vision of unity with every year of time and every tribe of his people, of movement and wandering children, rushing along past dead Polish cows and plundered villages, a great whirl of moving people, who, every few years, with pots and pans banging, picked up and moved on. This moving thing is in the blood, he thought. It is nothing to apologize for. What am I complaining about, I, whose relatives moved from the Bosporus and Black Sea to the Vistula and the Baltic? They were spat at, degraded, and robbed of their goods, but they kept going, enduring all so that I, Hiram Jaffe, could one day emerge unfettered and free to live in a rainbow-colored apartment painted by a man whose children brawl in the streets and whose ancestors burned

Jews at the stake during the *autos-da-fé*. History's logic is telepathic, he thought.

Just shut off your mind and paint that wall, you old Zoroastrian, you. The wall is all, and no funny stuff from the brain.

TWO

"Dolly?" he called, finding the door open but no wife
inside.

"I'm here at Andrea's," came the voice from above him.

The boxes were clustered just as he had left them, but
this didn't mean that they hadn't called to signal their
intentions. He took the stairs two at a time and burst
into the neighbor's apartment. Murphy skidded through
the door right behind him. "D'they call?"

"No one called while you were gone," his wife said.

"Hiram," said Andrea, "you've got green paint on your
head."

Deflated at the news that there had been no message,
Jaffe experienced a moment of reeling in his stomach. He
caught himself and in so doing realized that Andrea was
sitting there with her blouse off. She seemed to have three
breasts. He focused on the three breasts and discovered
that one of them was the bald head of Andrea's little
baby.

"I was just saying," Andrea noted, "that because you've got all your dishes and things packed you should have dinner up here tonight." The first thing that came into Jaffe's mind was putting a napkin around his neck and snuggling up to Andrea's breasts. That wasn't a nice thought at all, he told himself, but it was the way she said it. Andrea was a natural, corn-fed Kansas girl, and Jaffe considered her one of the ten friendliest, best-adjusted persons in North America.

"That's nice of you, but we wouldn't want to be a bother. You've got your hands full with the baby and everything."

"Honest, it's no trouble at all," she said, switching the baby from the left breast to the right. "I baked an apple pie this after. And Peter'll help with the dishes. He's out getting a few things at the grocer right now."

"The movers might come in the middle of everything and disrupt the meal," Jaffe replied.

"But I said they didn't call," Dolly observed.

"Doesn't mean they can't come without calling."

"Hiram," Andrea said, "let me get you a drink. You look like you need it."

Jaffe was about to protest but Andrea got up, baby fastened to her like suction, and went to a cabinet where with one hand she uncorked the top from a brandy bottle.

"Isn't she wonderful?" Dolly whispered. "She's so natural. It's so beautiful."

Andrea's long flaxen hair was plaited into a single long braid down the middle of her bare back. She must be some kind of a Kansas primitive, with a little Samoan blood somewhere on her mother's side, Jaffe thought.

27

"She's such a good mother. She's so capable. Look at how she does that," Dolly whispered. "If all mothers were like that," she added, "I'll bet Dr. Picker wouldn't have any business."

Jaffe didn't doubt that one bit, but he wondered what her husband would think if he walked in here and found Jaffe looking at his capable, half-naked Andrea, earth-mother or no earth-mother. Jaffe had a vision of Peter's response: Peter, a public school teacher, an affable, easy-going sort, and far from the kind to sock Jaffe in the eye, would say, "You marry a girl with Kansas breasts, and you really got something. These Midwest girls are built that way because they drink so many milkshakes when they're teen-agers."

That was one reason Jaffe didn't care for Peter. Dolly had justifiably accused him of being unfriendly to him. Apart from the fact that Peter had an explanation for everything, Jaffe's dislike really centered, in the more profound sense, on Peter's status as a public school teacher. Jaffe felt they were dangerous—teachers. They could ruin a kid for life and get off scot-free, with nobody knowing they were to blame. They could do more damage, Jaffe felt, than a doctor, and, worse, they didn't require all a doctor's fancy training. One woman, a Mrs. Goodpastor, had ruined Jaffe with numbers, back in the second or third grade somewhere. He didn't remember what or how, just that she somehow managed to panic him whenever it came to numbers. It was something that got progressively worse as the years went by. Once you got off on the wrong track with numbers you were finished. In high school and college, math courses gave him a wet, hot feeling in his bowels. The tension was so bad that before a math test he'd have terrible diarrhea and he would sit there on the toilet memorizing theorems and feel crowded by the big, rough penises drawn on the inside of the stalls. For as long as he remembered, he had had nightmares of grappling with impossible problems on math tests, dreams from which he awoke sweating and afraid. It had never stopped: when he was in London, the coinage nuisance entirely ruined the city for him, it had such a disturbing effect on him internally. He even needed an accountant for his meager income tax. It made him feel so foolish and incapable—and angry, too, because this very day Peter might have unknowingly implanted a *numbers* terror in some child's heart. And when Jaffe received the $2,000 option, he thought he'd invest some of it in the market and start a little something going; but he found himself utterly swamped by the confusion of the numbers and what they could do to him if he wasn't careful. It seemed impossible to Jaffe that thirty million Americans who owned stock understood so much more about numbers than he did. If they did, then he was living among a tribe of mathematical wizards, and he was hopelessly out of step with the times—outclassed, a great lummox of a mathematical moron.

The sound of a ringing phone downstairs jolted him from his daydreams. He took the staircase two steps at a time and caught the phone in his apartment on the third ring.

"Hiram, did you hear a report that Mickey Rooney and Arthur Godfrey were killed in a car accident?"

"What?"

"I heard it at the House of Chan last night. In the ladies' room. We had dinner."

It was his mother.

"No," he said, panting from the dash. "I didn't see anything in the paper today."

"And I didn't hear it on the radio."

"Then maybe it's not true. A rumor."

"We looked for it in the paper last night when we came out of the theater. Oh, the wind was terrible last night. I thought it would knock me off my feet. I thought I was going to have a heart attack. I said to Dad, 'This is it.' It was blowing so hard. He had to hold me up."

"Why didn't you take a taxi? Who said you had to walk around in the wind?"

"It was only from the House of Chan to the Radio City. Hiram?"

"What?"

"The picture at the Radio City was just beautiful. You ought to see it."

"Right."

"You and Dolly never go to the Radio City, do you?"

"No."

"It was lovely. It was about Israel."

"Right."

"We wouldn't have gone in all that wind but we bought tickets last month. Five dollars worth of tickets. I mean—we had to go."

"I know."

"How's the moving, Hiram?"

"What movie? I didn't go to the movies."

"Mov*ing*. I said m-o-v-i-n-g. I bet you could use some help."

"No, no. Everything's fine."

"Moving is such a terrible ordeal. . . ."

"I'm telling you, Mom, everything's fine."

"Well, when you're settled, we'll come down for dinner and have a look. Why, if you're moving, you don't get out of that neighborhood is beyond me. Thirty-five years ago that was *some* neighborhood. But now! The *element* there!"

"I'm your peculiar son. You tell me I do peculiar things."

"I don't like coming into that neighborhood. I really don't."

"I know what you mean. New York is filled with people who can run amuck any moment."

"Hiram, don't start anything. Don't give me that sarcasm of yours. Let this just be a quiet telephone call from your mother. Oh yes, before I forget, did you see that picture on the cover of last week's *Life?* Those college students with the signs, the demonstration in California?"

"Yes—."

"Was that you? The one on the right with the blue shirt? The girl looked like Dolly, too."

"I've never been in California."

"Well, I thought maybe they just said it was in California and the picture was New York. It certainly looks like you."

"Why would they lie?"

"I don't know. I just thought—."

"I have to go, Mom. Dolly needs me. She's stuck in a box."

"Hiram, just a minute. I want to tell you something. It's been on my mind. You know, when I speak to you on the phone you never ask about Dad, how he is or anything. That's not nice. It's like you're trying to cut yourself off."

"Do you ever ask about Dolly, Mom?"

"No. And I do it *intentionally*. I'm trying to show you how it feels."

"But *I* don't do it intentionally. Does that make it any better?"

"But it's not right. I mean, it hurts me when you don't ask. You have a father, and he's still alive, thank God."

"Mother, you know the answer but you won't admit it."

"What?"

"I'm a nasty kid. I always was. A no-good, rotten, dis-respectful, ungrateful, spiteful little bastard."

"Stop that. Oh, don't say that. I thought you were bet-ter. Oh, I hoped you were settling down."

"I'm fine."

"Oh, Hiram, I worry about you. What's going to hap-pen to you?"

"Mom, Dolly's legs are kicking like crazy. I've got to get her out of that box."

"Hiram—"

"She's struggling quite a bit."

"Hiram, I want to tell you to come up to our place for dinner if the moving is too much."

"Mom, if I don't get Dolly out, this very second . . ."

"All right, Hiram. Goodbye. But I don't know why you do this to yourself."

Damn phone, Jaffe thought. Here he was, at his age, still struggling with an unallayed parent problem, with old, unresolved grievances knocking around. It was so adolescent, but he couldn't turn it off. I don't need any calls like that today, he thought. What if I buzzed the telephone office again and asked them only to let through calls from the movers—no one else? No, they couldn't do that. Besides, it had become a very unexpected sort of day, one of the most unexpected he'd ever known, and he was afraid that all kinds of hell could follow from a request like that. He would never forgive himself for bringing in the phone company to make more trouble, just as his parents would never forgive him for not going into Dolly's father's business. Jaffe's obtuseness there seemed to them the height of stupidity, the zenith of blindness—a tragedy. It reflected on them, made them appear stupid in the eyes of the relatives: that they had failed as parents to instill proper values in their son; that they had raised some sort of freak simpleton who was incapable of seeing what was perfectly clear to everyone else—that if you marry the daughter of a department store owner, you're set for life, that if you don't go into the business ("You can write plays on the side, on Sundays, no?"), people think there's something wrong with you.

They were a lot more than just disappointed that he didn't go into the department store with Ben Korngold (a very big man in the Norfolk Jewish community). His parents truly envied the material success of Dolly's parents, their style of living—the house with the formica, all-electric kitchen; the swimming pool in the backyard; the shuffleboard in the finished basement; the trips to Europe (the Korngolds had been to Israel no less than four times, his parents not once); the month-long winter vacations at the pastel palaces in Miami Beach. They yearned, simply yearned, for the values that came so naturally to her parents.

Yet, he had noticed that his parents couldn't talk about their sons without bragging. Of Oscar, it was always, "Oh yes, he's doing very nicely. He knows all the high life. Pulls in some income, that boy." Hiram was the artistic one. "Writing pays good money. He once got a $2,000 option for a play. A very intelligent wife. Does psychiatric work. They raise dogs right here in the middle of the city." What did they have to boast about? He was an unsuccessful playwright and a hack writer at 30, and his brother was a prince among phonies, a divorced, neurotic, selfish philistine. "Four years of college, the way we deprived ourselves," his mother lamented to him recently. "For this—a dog walker. It's pretty tough for a parent to take, believe me. One day you'll be a parent and you'll understand." Jaffe knew, to his wonderment, that in the next instant the phone could ring and she could get on the line with a friend and begin boasting about him.

Dinner at his parents' house could completely undo him on a day like this. He'd go into their bathroom to wash his hands, and the medicine chest door would swing open as he turned the tap—just as it had for all the years when he lived there. His mind lapsed back to that emotional moment when he had gazed into their medicine chest last month. A sad, woozy feeling had invaded him, a heaviness of pain that choked him in the throat. Their mineral oil, tablet laxatives, heartburn pills, antacid suckers, chalky anti-ulcer lozenges, mouthwash, sedatives, sleeping pills,

34

and two whole shelves of brown-bottled pills, each containing a slightly different shaped pill that was to affect the iron, the liver, the circulation, the digestion, the gas, the joints, the nerves, the buzzing in the ears, the palpitating of the heart, the fuzziness of the sight and the scratchiness of the throat. Nothing so simple as an aspirin existed for them. To soothe their special kind of aggravation, more complex remedies must be always at hand. Devils, real or imagined, struck obscure diseases into every part of their bodies. Hiram, transfixed at the medicine chest, couldn't fail to see himself as their chief aggravator—an irresponsible role to assume, Dolly told him, assuring her husband that Dr. Picker would also have found his conclusion shortsighted. Later on, it occurred to Jaffe how beautiful it would be if he opened that medicine chest and found there was just a bottle of bees' honey or a clump of all-purpose moss. It was painful but he couldn't help think what a different person he'd be today if he had had parents who kept nothing but moss in their medicine chest.

The ringing phone made him jump.

"Mr. Jaffe?"

"Yes?"

"Movers here." It was the flighty girl. "I heard from the boss."

"Yes?"

"I'm afraid there'll be some delay."

"Till what time?"

"He's not sure he can make it at all today."

"He's not sure? What does that mean? Can he or can't he?"

"Maybe at nine o'clock or so—if the move they're on now continues without a hitch. He had one of the longest delays in the company's history."

"Tell me where he is. Why can't I speak to him? Why do the messages have to be relayed like this?"

"I gave you the message. What else is there?"

"But I . . . I don't have a clear picture in my mind. If I could speak to him directly—I mean, for example, upon what does it depend whether or not he gets here tonight. And if it's going to be after eight o'clock, I don't know whether they'll let us move in at the other building that late. And if it's tomorrow, what time, tomorrow? I have to know these things because people are supposed to move in here. I'm not supposed to be here any more."

"You're exaggerating."

"What do you mean I'm exaggerating? Look Miss, what's your name, anyway?"

"Myrna. I'm the boss's woman."

"Where can I reach the boss, Myrna? Where is he at now? I'd just like to talk to him myself. You passed on the message beautifully, honest to God you did. But I'd just like to speak to him."

"I don't know where he is."

"You don't know? How is that possible?"

"I know the party's old address where he's moving them *from*, but I don't know where it's going. He's already moved them out, so there's nobody there to answer."

"But there must be an order thing in the office saying where the stuff is going to. Could you look at that and tell me where it's going?"

"I'm afraid that's impossible."

36

"Why?"

"I'm afraid I can't tell you that."

"Dammit, I don't understand how you run your business."

"That's the secret of our success. Low overhead and less paper work."

"It isn't fair. The system works for everyone else, why not for me?"

"I think you're exaggerating again, Mister."

Jaffe went limp. For a moment he couldn't think of another question to ask. Then one occurred to him. "Could you ask him to call me the next time you speak to him? If you're worried about the overhead, tell him to bill me for the phone call."

"I don't expect to be hearing from him again. I'll be going to sleep soon."

"Sleep? It's only six o'clock."

"If you don't mind, I'm a little tired. Do I have to explain my personal life to you? I was up all last night. One of the regular men was out."

"You mean you were doing the moving? Lifting boxes and furniture?"

"Sure. The boss taught me how. It's all a matter of knowing how to bend. I carried my first upright yesterday."

"You did not. What do you hope to gain by telling me something like that? I don't believe any of this."

"Whaddya wise or something, Mister? I ought to know whether I carried it or not."

"How tall are you?"

"Five-four."

"How much do you weigh?"

"Hundred fifteen. I'm thirty-six, twenty-six, thirty-six, but that's got nothing to do with it. The bending's the important thing. Anybody in the business'll tell you that."

"You must be muscular, that's the only explanation."

"In the backs of my legs I'm quite powerful. I can take most guys in Indian leg-wrestling."

"Now you're just bragging."

"It tightens your stomach, too. The boss and I exchange socks in the stomach and I hardly feel a thing."

"You're married to a man who punches you in the stomach?"

"It's only a game."

"What about your reproductive organs? You could do yourself permanent harm."

"They're way inside. It's nothing to get excited about. He hits high in the gut, where the muscles are, not down in the breadbasket."

"You tell your husband he's got to stop punching you in the stomach. I'll tell him so myself when I see him."

"You mean *if* you get to see him."

"What do you mean by that?"

"I'm going to tell him about the way you've been talking to me."

"What have I said that's so terrible? You're married to a man who puts pianos on your back and punches you in the stomach and mere *words* offend you?"

"You been practically calling me a liar. I'm going to tell him that."

"No, no. It's just that what you said sounded so strange. But I believe you. Honestly, I believe every word of it."

"You're just saying that because you're afraid the boss won't want to do the move, once he hears how you've been insulting me."

"Myrna, what can I say? I speak to you as one human being to the next. Don't reveal to your husband the contents of this conversation. I appeal to your sense of compassion."

There was a pause, then she said in a new, soft, voice, "I like that. Especially the second part. You're a writer, aren't you?"

Jaffe felt a flutter in his stomach. "Then it's agreed?"

"I think we understand each other now, Mr. Jaffe."

"God bless you, Myrna."

"So long, Mr. Jaffe."

Abruptly, the panicky feeling inside him gave way to excitement. He wanted to meet Myrna. He wondered whether tomorrow she might come along and lift his piano. Maybe she'd let him feel the backs of her legs when she did that.

Dolly opened the door.

"She's wonderful."

"Myrna?"

"Andrea. With the baby. Who's Myrna?"

"I meant Andrea. I forgot her name for the moment."

"She's got such good instincts with that kid. I mean, she hardly ever reads or anything. She just knows what to do with that baby. It's beautiful, it really is. You can tell there'll never be any incest in that family."

"Incest?" Jaffe exclaimed. "Who said anything about incest?"

39

"Oh, I've got it in my mind. This woman came to see Dr. Picker yesterday and she was a nudist. Her husband was too. They had made nudists out of their children even. They're teen-agers. Everyone walks around their house with no clothes on. Even their grandparents, when they come over for a visit: zip, no clothes. Three generations walking around bare-assed, eating ice cream. They go on summer vacations to nudist colonies. Anyhow, all of a sudden, after years of this business, the woman starts to worry about incest."

Jaffe, fascinated, made a circling motion with two fingers. "Wait a minute, you're going too fast. Which way? With whom?"

"She wasn't clear about that on the first visit. Dr. Picker thinks it's interesting because he says you don't get much incest in New York these days. Who called?"

"My mother."

"She didn't want to speak to *me*, did she?"

"Of course not."

"Just let me become pregnant and we'll see how interested she becomes in my welfare."

"By the way, the movers called again."

Dolly lit a cigarette. Jaffe waited for his wife to ask what the mover had to say, but she didn't. He didn't feel that was natural.

"Did they put your mind at rest?" she asked, exhaling.

"Just don't be so solicitous about my mind. They're still not sure if they can make it tonight. Maybe tomorrow. I expect to hear from them again. Apparently there was some problem with the move they had earlier in the day."

"You get such cheap movers. If you would have spent

40

a few more dollars you could have gotten someone reliable, someone who's at least listed in the Yellow Pages,
and then we wouldn't have had all this trouble. My father
would have given us the extra money."

Jaffe didn't feel that this was worth answering.

"If the idea of my father paying the extra mover money
upsets you, why don't you get an advance from Asch
against your next sale?"

Still Jaffe didn't feel obliged to answer.

Dolly went right on. "You're crippled when it comes
to spending money, and you can't help yourself. It's your
parents' fault. They did that to you."

"Dolly, do me a favor and get a job in an insurance
company, will you? A secretary in a paper clip factory or
something."

She turned to face him with a look that said it all: I'm
twenty-five and motherless. He knew the expression well.
Get me with child, and the job at Dr. Picker's ends.
Jaffe felt *she* felt that this was the chief reason they were
moving to a bigger apartment—the space for a family.
That was her secret hope, he knew: for her, the moving
had nothing to do with the repellent laborers, the jackhammers, the petitioners, the mailbox crammed with soul-
ful letters from Jerusalem orphanages. No. To her, the
larger apartment meant inhabiting it, furnishing the empty
corners with cribs and babies. Never mind about suffocat-
ing an artist in his prime. Babies were more important
than art. He reasoned slyly: once he got her out of here,
away from this Andrea, her baby fixation would surely
temper.

"Andrea was telling me," Dolly began, in a falsely

41

academic voice, "that Indians carried their babies in pouches stuffed with moss."

"I thought you said Andrea doesn't read books."

"There was an Indian reservation in northern Michigan where she worked one summer."

"That's funny, because I was just thinking about moss."

"Certainly not about babies," she said.

"Oh yes, babies too. They're quite the food for thought these days."

"The nursing part is very important. Too many mothers use formulas, and that deprives the child of the sucking pleasure. Very few breast-fed babies ever become thumb-suckers or pacifier-obsessives."

"Is that so?" said Jaffe.

"Unless they're being breast-fed and it suddenly stops —a traumatically rapid transition from the breast to the bottle. Sometimes that will make a thumb-sucker out of a baby."

Jaffe read her voice clearly: there was in it not so much jealousy, but cool, knifing anger. Then, abruptly, Jaffe had a vision: it was of a Passover *seder* at his father's house. The old man had tears in his eyes from looking at his grandson, five years old, sitting there with a *yarmulka* on his head in front of all the beautiful silver and white linen. It was, he felt, a vision of perfect truth: but was that *all* the baby business meant? Is that all there was to life? Somehow, Jaffe couldn't see himself at that table with his son. It was too corny an idea; he would feel cheated. There must be more to babies than nonsense like that.

"Andrea said her pediatrician was different than the other doctors who—"

42

"I'm sure she said different *from*, considering the fact her husband is a teacher. I shouldn't think he'd let her get away with saying different *than*, unless of course you don't remember whether, in truth, she actually said—"

"*Stop* it."

"Dolly, I want to tell you something. What truly worries me, what absolutely unsettles me, is this: what happens the day the kid comes to me—say he's fourteen—and says, 'What's the point of living?' Or 'What's the meaning of life?' Now what the hell am I supposed to tell him? Couldn't his entire relationship with his father depend on my success or failure with the right words at that moment? I'm the kind of person who could easily live in dread of that moment for fourteen years. I mean it, what am I supposed to tell him? Will I have an answer ready by then?"

Dolly threw up her hands. "But we don't even have a son yet. How can you even begin to think about something like that?"

Ignoring her remark, Jaffe went on: "What do other guys do when their kids ask that type of question?"

Dolly was shouting: "The other guys don't *worry* about it. That's the difference between *you* and the other guys."

For a moment Jaffe seemed to smart under the utter simplicity of her answer. But no, he realized, that was much too easy. He looked at her standing there and pleaded with his mind to look at the world the way she did, on just this one subject, at least. It was not only that she wanted to win him over to her viewpoint, regarding a family, but she wanted to help him, to straighten out what she considered an unhealthy attitude. That was her

43

benignly helpful side, and no more than he could control unreasonable stinginess she couldn't control being helpful. The other day he had come home, turned the radio on, and heard something about a flood in Ohio. Dolly should have been home, but she wasn't, and he immediately fantasied her hearing about the flood, rushing off in a helicopter and flying to the nearest disaster area. She'd come back in a week with a Negro baby swaddled in her arms and say, "I'm keeping the baby for six months just so he'll stay out of the hospital. They disintegrate in an institution. They need mother love."

"Here," said Jaffe, revolving an orange in his hands, "is another point of departure between us. Just the other day I heard that very often when oranges are picked they're really green and that they're sprayed afterward with an orange dye." He sighed sadly. "Can we believe something like that about oranges? If I asked them, would the Sunkist people admit it? Do you," and he pointed an accusing finger at his wife, "feel anything about such an idea one way or another?"

Dolly exhaled exasperation. "A sensitive person like you who thinks continually—and I *know* you think continually —is in danger of going mad."

"That's nonsense, Dolly. It's healthy thinking, usually."

"No. All the evidence says that continual thinking cannot be healthy. Only limited thinking is healthy."

"Okay, Dolly, where did you read that? What propaganda magazine?"

"One day—*poom!*—and you'll have a cerebral explosion."

"No, no, no. There'll be no cerebral explosions. Only

a running down of tired parts from time to time. I don't see anything so dramatic as an explosion."

"That's because you don't know how it works."

"And neither does Dr. Picker for that matter," he snapped.

"Who said anything about Dr. Picker?"

"You did, Dolly. *Your* voice, but his ideas."

"*My* ideas. *Mine.* Don't you give me credit for any original thoughts?"

"Of course I do. That's why I married you."

"I thought it was for my body."

"That too. That's very important."

"But lately it's only a little important, right? Lately, in fact, I find myself wondering *why* you married me. All you do is criticize."

"I've got to go out."

"But I want to talk. That's not fair."

"Why don't I carry the radio over to the new apartment. I'll take the picture of Vishtaspa, too."

"*Damn* you," she cried, "and your goddam Zoroastrian gods."

45

THREE

Jaffe met Peter at the entrance to the building, Peter all tall and straw-headed, as square in his head as he was lean in his height.

"Hi!" Peter called brightly, as though there was more than three feet between him and Jaffe. "Moving some stuff, are ya?"

"Just a couple of things. You know—that the movers might break."

"Movers. Gee, why'd you get movers? I'd have helped you. We could've rented a little truck—"

"We have that piano and that big couch. Especially for the piano, though, you need someone who knows what he's doing."

Peter shook his head. "All the same, I'll bet we coulda done the job."

Jaffe winced inside as Peter pronounced "job" like *jab*.

"Who's the picture of the guy with the beard?"

"Oh, that's Vishtaspa, father of Darius."

The cord on the picture was digging into his fingers and Jaffe changed his grip. He was aware that Peter was smiling at him good-naturedly, all expectant and benevolent. He was every bit as friendly as his wife Andrea, and Jaffe considered it something fateful that they had found each other, these two friendly young people.

"It's a pity you're moving, now that the girls were just beginning to get on so well together. I know Andrea thinks the world of Dolly."

"Yes," Jaffe picked up, figuring that for just this last time with Peter he would return banality for banality, "and Dolly thinks the world of Andrea. She's mad for your baby, too." Jaffe thought to himself: what's the goddam kid's name again?

Peter chuckled a proud father's laugh. "John's a great little guy." It occurred to Jaffe that he never did know what part of the provinces Peter came from; someplace very remote, he thought, where they called eight-week-old infants *Jan.*

Peter hefted a long package and said, "Well—."

Something about the shape of the thing bothered Jaffe.

"Andrea'll be glad to see this. We had a notice for it from the post office. I got there just before they closed."

"What is it?"

"Andrea's gun," Peter said matter-of-factly.

Jaffe was amazed. What does one of the friendliest wholesomest girls in America need with a gun?

"Andrea's a sharpshootress," Peter said. "Didn't you ever see her scrapbook? I suppose not. If we'd have known each other better, I suppose she'd have brought

47

it out. She's kind of shy sometimes. She was a junior state champion."

"Formidable," Jaffe said. "But what's she going to do with the gun upstairs?"

"It's just kind of reassuring to have it around. She doesn't have any plans for coming out of retirement, yet, if you know what I mean. I thought it would be a good idea to have a gun in the house. Andrea couldn't use it on a person, I don't think. *I* could, though. I really could. One of these junkies might come fooling around at the lock, and I've got a family inside. You know, you've got a right to protect your loved ones. Back home, of course, I'd never think of anything like that. People are different there."

It was about all Jaffe could stand. He hefted his radio and painting. "Say, would you mind opening the door?" he asked Peter.

Out on the street, Jaffe heard the piano music drifting out from the top floor. It came from that old man's apartment, the Lithuanian who gave piano lessons up there. He was someone Jaffe had wanted to get to know, but the man hardly ever went out; the old Lithuanian had too much trouble with the four flights of stairs. He had developed into something of a mystery because, when he thought about it, Jaffe couldn't figure out what the hell Lithuanians knew about piano playing in the first place. But it was the superintendent who had originally put the ethnic peg on the piano teacher, and it occurred to Jaffe that the super, being as dumb as he was, might have

48

gotten it mixed up: he might have meant to say Babylonian, not Lithuanian.

Jaffe smiled at the thought, and kept right on smiling until he passed a boy, maybe ten years old, weaving across the sidewalk, absorbed in a comic book. He was a mopey-looking child, lumpy-fattish, a boy who, Jaffe knew, would have a whining sound in his voice, and sweat terribly in a game of stickball. What if I had a kid who looked like that? Jaffe had a frightful moment. You struggle to raise a son, take on extra work to meet the bills, compromise yourself all over the place, undertake all kinds of disgusting work—only to father a third-rate sort of kid. Then again, maybe that would be a blessing: a satisfied, secure child who asked no questions of the universe. A blessing? No, a curse. A kid like that would be a dullard. The kid would submit to anything. How could they communicate with each other? He knew the answer: they couldn't, and thus the father-son cycle of inhumanity to each other would be renewed, as nature intended it.

"Dammit," Jaffe swore. Now why did I think that? What good does it do? What brings it on?

It was the moving, he knew. It was having some kind of effect on him. And it was Dolly, and all this baby bullshit. Creeping into his mind had come a kind of presentiment, a knowledge of something about to happen that maybe should best not happen, especially in the chaotic condition he was in. He was not adequately prepared, not ready. Assuming they got the environment part working perfectly for the kid, what about the heredity? Look at what the kid would have in his blood, what he couldn't control. Jaffe's parents: no point crying about that again. Dolly's parents: the kid's chromosomes would be shaped like dollar signs. It was utterly bizarre how her parents' every conversation seemed to lead into and end with money. If you get off the track, talking about a good movie (that had happened the last time they had seen them), Ben Korngold would put his head down and nod: nod, nod, nod, as if he knew all about that aesthetic crap. And then someone would say, well, it had been playing at this theater in New York for four months, and suddenly Ben Korngold would snap to, his senses prickling: "There you are—you see—at say 300 people a night, $2.50 a ticket, then you figure the distributor's cut and the theater owner gets a good percentage, still they must be pulling it in, an Italian company you say, they're sharp businessmen, don't let anyone kid you, we've got a line of quality Italian leather gloves, two hundred dollars a dozen, would you believe it?" He absolutely relished talking money business: there was love in his voice when he talked money. Respect. Awe. Ben Korngold was in love with money. Beautiful money, business money, gross and net money, big successful money. Money came to life when he talked about it.

His father-in-law's attitude made Jaffe feel very conspicuous without money. And although Ben Korngold was a perfect moron on any subject except money, he always seemed to dominate the conversation and bring it around to his favorite interest. There were meals at the Korngolds when the money-talk made Jaffe absolutely nauseous, making Jaffe pick at his food, making Ben Korngold shoot his wife a questioning look as though to say, "Look at this man our Dolly married. He eats like a bird. What's the matter with him?" Afterward, Dolly would apologize to Jaffe for her father's money talk, explaining how he was very poor as a boy, that he never had had anything and was still insecure and that's why he talked about it so much. "I didn't know explanations like that were still valid," Jaffe told her the last time, and yet it didn't stop him from knowing also that the money would make all the difference, that if he'd made a quarter-million on a Broadway play or a Hollywood sale that then his father-in-law would find food-picking justified and understand-able: the boy is worried about high stakes, a big trans-action, money-thinking.

His mother-in-law was not quite as thick as the old man. In a moment of intuition she had observed to her daughter: "Sometimes I think Hiram believes that be-cause people have a lot of money they can't be good people." She should have stopped there, but instead at-tempted to overwhelm her daughter with the naïvité of Hiram's view by posing the stunner: "And what about the people with money who give to charitable causes? How does he answer that?" Jaffe's mother-in-law was also a bit on the grasping side. He never thought she was nasty in the least. Just abysmally shallow: narrow-minded in the extreme.

It was apocalyptic, the genes of such people in his child. Worse, it was unjust, a cruelty.

When he returned to the brownstone, the door to the back apartment on the first floor was open. Gupta, with his long, bony, squid-like Indian arms, was standing there frowning.

"Truly, truly, Hiram, I am sorry to see you moving. I will genuinely miss our fine discussions."

Jaffe smiled.

Gupta continued to frown.

"It's only a couple of blocks," Jaffe said, impatient to get upstairs to see if the movers had called while he was out.

"Yes, but here it was as though we were all branches on the same tree."

Jaffe recalled that once before Gupta had described the tenants in the building as fruit in the same garden. Gupta was from a solid family, his father an economist with the Indian government in New Delhi, Gupta himself a graduate student at Columbia University. Recently, Jaffe's friendship with Gupta had experienced a strain; it followed when Spiegler was caught refusing to show an empty apartment to a Negro couple. Gupta sided with Spiegler in the moral arguments that followed, explaining to Jaffe a theory about caste and segregation that seemed to work fine for the Guptas of New Delhi. "What a snob," Dolly had said, and, as though to prove the point, Gupta's famous episode with his Buddhist friend shook the building about a week later. His friend, with whom he had once gone to school in India, was in the city on a visit from M.I.T., and, the day he left, he gave Gupta a bottle of offering. Late for his plane, he had received Gupta's promise to dispense with the bottle by throwing it into the Hudson River, from where it would glide out into the eternal waters. The bottle contained parts of their dinner,

some wine, ginger ale, curry sauce, a few pieces of pista-
chio nut. Gupta left the bottle in the bathroom, forgotten,
and while he was out one afternoon there ensued an explosion that shattered the bathroom window. The fire
department came and axed down Gupta's door. Gupta
returned from his afternoon class to face a cross-examina-
tion by the police and fire department about whether
he was operating a still, his apartment dense with the
smell of fermented wine. Gupta was humiliated. "These
Buddhists," he hissed later.

Now Gupta stood there in slippers with his perennial
toothbrush, dabbing thoughtfully at a molar, a bicuspid.
"Yes, I will miss our discussions," he said, making Jaffe
think of Tagore, emancipated women, birth control, and
the Kama Sutra—Gupta's favorite subjects.

"Cut it out, Gupta. I'm only moving a couple of blocks.
It's not like I'm dying or something."

Gupta shook his head solemnly. "You must be careful
about flux, Hiram. Seek the other thing."

"Ah Gupta," Jaffe cried, heading for the stairs, remembering what Dolly always said, that what Gupta needed
was to get laid.

"Any calls?"
"None," Dolly replied.
"None?"
"Well, one."
Jaffe waited: good news, bad news? Why did she try
to hide it?
"It was a wrong number. Somebody Spanish."
"Oh."

Murphy was rubbing her bulk about Jaffe's leg. Jaffe gave her two heavy thuds on the rear and her tail responded with instant happiness.

"Do you want anything to eat?" Dolly asked.

Jaffe shrugged. "I don't think so."

"Maybe we could go out for something. It would be easier," she said, nodding at the confusion of boxes which held their food, pans, plates, and silverware.

"I'm really not hungry. Besides, we might miss them."

"They're never going to come. You ought to make some other arrangements in the morning."

"Don't say that, Dolly. They're coming. If not tonight, then tomorrow. I had a long talk with the girl in the office, before."

"Is that who Myrna is?"

"Yeah, that's Myrna."

Dolly put her hand over her stomach. "No kidding," she said, "I'm hungry. Can't we get something fast outside?"

"I told you I wasn't hungry. If you want to go, then go."

"Hiram, won't you ever learn?"

"Learn what?"

"That you can't exist on V-8 juice and Oreos?"

"No such thing as can't."

"There is *too* such a thing as can't. That's a popular misconception. I read that just recently."

"Where? In a book? I once read a book."

"I *know* how much you've been eating this week. It's not healthy."

"Dolly, for Chrissake, you make it sound like Oreos and

54

V-8 juice are *all* I've been eating. I've had quite a few peanut butter and jelly sandwiches and vichysoisse soup lunches."

"That's awful." She wrinkled her face.

"You're just jealous because I've got good taste."

"Taste? *Murphy* eats better than you."

"I should hope so."

"Why?"

"She's got purer blood in her veins than I. She's the result of selective breeding. She deserves better."

"That's foolish. . . . You know, sometimes you remind me of the story about the scientist and the centipede."

"What story?"

"About the scientist who said to the centipede, 'Good Lord, how can you walk without getting all those legs tangled up?' And that made the centipede so self-conscious that he became tangle-footed from then on."

"No kidding!"

The phone rang. Jaffe jumped to it so quickly that Murphy barked, startled.

Somebody said a few words in Spanish. There was noise, loud music in the background.

"You must have the wrong number," Jaffe said.

"Isn't Joe there?" asked the voice.

"Joe who?"

"Joe, I work wit heem in the factory. I dono hees las name."

"No, I'm telling you there's no Joe. Nobody here works in a factory. Check the number, okay?"

The voice gave a mocking laugh. "Okay."

"Did yours ask for Joe?" he asked Dolly.

55

She nodded. "Our Spanish friend again?"

"I wonder if it's that wise guy at the phone company," Jaffe said, a hint of anxiety in his eyes. "We hardly ever get the wrong num——"

The phone rang again, and Jaffe's hand was still on it. "Hello?"

"Joe?" This time it was a woman's voice.

"No. Now look, would you mind checking that ——"

"Come on," the woman said, "lemmee speaka Joe." Beyond the earpiece were the same background sounds, chattering voices and Latin American music.

"Now look, I'm expecting an important call, so please try to check that number."

"Why you no lemmee speaka Joe?" the woman asked, and this time Jaffe heard a lilt, a light laugh in her voice.

"Miss, if you don't stop this, I'm going to have the phone company trace these calls."

"Hey, you can' do that. There's no such thing. And besides—."

"Besides what?"

"You do that an' I get Joe after you," she laughed.

Jaffe slammed the phone down. "Goddamit, why is this machine working against me today? All I want is one simple positive call and I get these lunatics calling up." Suddenly his body snapped out of his chair.

"Hiram, for heaven's sake! What's the matter?"

"The new apartment's going to be robbed. Don't you see?" He stood wide-eyed, as though confronting a vision. "They put the new phone in there this morning. It has the same number. It may be the painter's doing, or maybe the painter's wife, or maybe one of his kids. I brought the television over there this morning and a suitcase filled with manuscripts. Somebody saw the television and the suitcase and figured, maybe because of the paint smell, that we may not be there tonight. They're checking to see if we're there. If we're here, we can't be there. It's the old bit. But maybe they don't know that the phone is still connected here. So it's ringing in both places, get it?"

"Hiram, now you just stop it."

"No, that's it. Don't you see?"

"It's your imagination. Just because we get a couple of wrong numbers. It's only a coincidence."

"I'm going to get my hands on a couple of nasty dogs and go over."

"Hiram, don't."

"Yes, I'll leave Murphy here. I don't want a fainting dog on my hands."

"Get Peter to go with you."

"Peter's having dinner."

"Gupta."

"Gupta's brushing his teeth."

As he left, Jaffe heard Dolly's lament: "Hiram, you're not saying any of the right things today."

He would get Omar, the Saluki, and then hop across the street for the Katzes' German shepherd. They're a pair of dogs to reckon with. The two of them together would destroy a lion if a lion started getting wise with them. Downstairs, Jaffe rounded the corner and entered the Spanish grocery. A box of biscuits for the dogs would be just the thing, in case they got nervous. The grocer was ladeling out cereal from a big sack. Over the radio

57

an hysterical announcer was doing a baseball game from somewhere in Puerto Rico. Jaffe turned to the dark boy behind the counter but his eyes seemed to get stuck on a picture above him, on the shelf next to the ragged line of *Goya* canned goods. The words went slack in Jaffe's mouth. The picture showed Christ standing with his arms out, rays of garish, faded sun, painted in muddy shades of red and gold, spraying out in the background. What alarmed Jaffe was the newspaper photo portrait of John Kennedy in the picture's left-hand corner. It was as though the grocer had decided that his omission from the original picture was an oversight, that the artist, given the chance again, would have painted Kennedy into that tableau of Christ and shooting rays. Jaffe had been in the store a hundred times and never noticed it before. Why did he see it tonight?

Outside, shifting the box of biscuits from one hand to the next, Jaffe looked at himself in the black glass between the grocery and the tailor shop. A little frantic, he thought. Distraught; not so youthful as I feel. But at least I'm not talking to myself. The sewing machine behind the glass was idle, resting in the dark, while the tailor, Kaminsky, rested himself upstairs. What I need is a really good tailor, Jaffe thought: a spiritual tailor. Someone who can do alterations on my soul.

Five floors above West End Avenue, Mrs. Katz opened the door. She looked surprised. Jaffe had rehearsed it on the elevator, and he reeled off an enthusiastic story about a friend of his who was interested in mating his female shepherd, and Jaffe had told him that the handsomest male in the city lived just a couple of blocks away and would Mrs. Katz let him take the dog off to his place for a few minutes so his friend could have a look. Jaffe told her there was money in it, and also her choice of the litter.

Mrs. Katz was flattered, but she asked, "Why couldn't your friend come over here?"

Jaffe nodded, having anticipated the question. "He was in a motor scooter accident recently and he's got a few bad ligaments. He's using a crutch this evening." Mrs. Katz nodded. "His dog's coming into heat next week. He's really very interested."

"Here," Mrs. Katz said, giving Jaffe the leash, "you take Hansie right over. I hope your friend likes him. And your friend's dog, too."

Across the street, Jaffe tied Hans to the back stairway and spread out a fist full of biscuits. He used the same pitch—a friend whose Saluki was coming into heat—on Mrs. Simon. It worked just as perfectly.

Heading up the street, Omar attached to his right hand, Hans to his left, Jaffe felt like a heroic sheriff in a bad Western. Instead of a pair of sixshooters, he was packing a pair of fangs. Instead of an army of gunslingers out there, it was a showdown with the Spanish underworld.

The doorman at his new building made an incredulous face and said, "All those dogs belong to you?" The apparent reference included Murphy, whom the doorman had observed with Jaffe earlier in the day.

Ignoring the question, Jaffe asked, "Have you been here all the time for the last hour?" The doorman looked from one dog to the next and then, as though deciding he had better be honest, replied, "Well, I went down to the cellar once to take a piss."

Jaffe hit the elevator button and the doors drew back. "That's all I wanted to know."

"What the hell's going on?" the doorman asked.

"Maybe nothing," Jaffe said. As the doors began to close, he added, "but maybe somebody's going to get mangled in just a couple of minutes."

At the door to his apartment on the penultimate floor, Jaffe stood silently and listened. Both dogs had their noses to the crack in a vacuum-like, scent-seeking ritual. He shifted Omar's leash to his left hand, and decided to do it quickly. He plunged the key in, spun the lock, and threw the door open.

He had meant to hold both dogs on their leashes, but as soon as the door opened they rushed in with such violence that Jaffe was unable to hold on. Both were barking, tearing from one room to the next, skidding on the bare wooden floors. Their cries echoed savagely in the empty apartment.

Jaffe felt for a switch and flipped it. There was no light. He moved along the wall toward a point where he remembered another switch. Nothing happened with that one either.

He returned to the front door and opened it, bringing a beam of light into the foyer. He was pleased that the door stayed open by itself.

Jaffe went into the bedroom to check the closet. It was open and empty. Fur flew past his legs. He couldn't tell whose, Omar or Hans. Just as casually he walked back to the front closet, and opened the door. A hand flew out

60

and Jaffe felt an abrupt shakiness at the side of his head. It felt more like the heel of a hand than a fist. There was a moment of metal flashing in the air, Jaffe jumping backward, and then a figure, either shorter than he or in a crouch, dashing for the door. The sound of running feet brought the dogs charging. A hand whipped at the door, slamming it shut just as the figure passed through it, and Hans sailed into the door, two feet over the floor, and made a brutal, crashing noise. Omar arrived, enraged, and clawed at the door.

Touching his head to make sure that it was not wet or open, that nothing metal had struck him, Jaffe at the same time walked a tentative two steps to check his balance. He surprised himself by managing to think the very clear thought that if he opened the door the two dogs would surely pounce on the man in seconds and could quite likely kill him. Jaffe decided not to open the door, unsure of his reasoning, whether death by mangling was too great a price for the burglar to pay, or whether he wasn't in the mood for any new kind of hilarity, with policemen and detectives asking a million questions. Instead, he calmed the dogs, showering them with caresses and biscuits.

While they were eating, Jaffe checked on the radio, the television set, and his manuscript-laden suitcase. He was only able to find one light bulb in its socket—in the kitchen. Even the bulb over the bathroom sink was missing.

When five minutes later his heart stopped beating like a fire engine, he took the leashes in hand and left his new apartment, confident that no one would bother the place again that night. But when he looked at Hans in the hall-way light, he realized he had to return to the apartment again to perform an ablution on him.

Mrs. Katz said: "Well?"

"Well what?" Jaffe asked.

"Did your friend like him?"

"Loved him. They really hit it off."

Mrs. Katz's nostrils twitched. "I smell turpentine."

"I don't smell anything," said Jaffe.

"Why does Hansie smell from turpentine?" she asked, her voice a little higher.

"I recommend you give him a bath, Mrs. Katz. A dog that's gone without a bath too long starts smelling a little turpy after a while. It's a chemical reaction in the coat follicles." Jaffe hoped that in rubbing the dog down in the kitchen, he had gotten off all the green paint. He could explain a turpentine smell, but green paint was something else.

"I never heard of such a thing."

"Ask any vet," Jaffe suggested. "Good night now."

"I thought you were reliable," Mrs. Katz said.

"I am, I am."

FOUR

Murphy whined at the smell of male dogs on Jaffe's pants.

"Dolly, you wouldn't believe it," Jaffe was saying. "The people who moved out took all the light bulbs. One bulb left in the whole place. What poor manners the former tenants must have had. To do something like that. What bad sports."

"Did you catch any burglars?"

"No, I let him get away. He was there, all right."

"He was not. You're making it up."

Jaffe smiled knowingly at the picture passing before him, snarling dogs and an adventure at the closet. It was as if he had drawn a measure of strength from the encounter, a physical thing ordinarily foreign to his make-up. He inhaled a self-satisfied breath, a sharp hint of pungency, the turpentine, still fresh on his hands. But wasn't it something else, too? Something like pipe tobacco smoke?

"It was exciting," Jaffe commented.

"He certainly was."

"Who?"

"The mover. He was here."

"I *thought* I smelled the tobacco smoke. Where is he? What did he say?"

"Well, he's pretty sorry about everything, but he can't make it today anymore." Dolly said it with no hint of suspense, of anything out of the ordinary. But then, Jaffe knew, she was generously straightforward about most things.

"Tomorrow's a possibility, but the hitch there is that he has a move scheduled for the morning and afternoon. He said that if he rushes he *might* be able to get here by five or six o'clock. But he warned us that his men would be exhausted by that hour and that they wouldn't be operating at peak efficiency or anything. He said there are usually more damage claims that arise out of the second or third move in a day than the first. But if he can't make it Saturday, then it would be Sunday definitely."

The danger-drawn excitement that had visited Jaffe fled with the mover news. He felt plunged right back into deepest anxiety. "So tomorrow's definitely out?"

"Not definitely. Probably."

Jaffe had a hundred questions, but knew none of them could be answered absolutely. He wanted a straight answer, so he asked, "Was his wife with him?"

"You mean he's married?" Dolly asked, surprised.

"What's that got to do with anything?" Jaffe wanted to know.

"*You* brought it up."

64

"And why shouldn't I? Just tell me, was she here with him or wasn't she?"

"Oh, I get it. Myrna's his wife."

"That's right. Myrna."

"No. We were alone. He didn't mention anything about a wife. You should see him, though. He has a big red beard. He smokes a pipe. And he's so virile-looking. Muscles and everything. He said he thought he knew you from college."

Jaffe's eyes closed for a moment. "Dolly," he said tiredly, "it's been a bad day. That's enough now. Quit handing me this shit about the mover being here."

Dolly protested in a voice that seemed genuine to Jaffe. "But it's true. I'm simply telling you the truth. It's as true as your story about the dogs chasing a burglar out of our new apartment."

"But that *is* true."

"So's what I'm telling you about the mover."

"Okay. What else?" he said in a humoring, flat voice.

"Well," Dolly said, looking off at a distant box across the room, summoning up images and details, "he was apologetic to me about all the inconvenience. He thought you were being kept posted by his office on a more regular basis. You know, an hour-to-hour account. He said the last thing he'd want to do is intentionally keep someone like me in the dark. He said it kind of funny."

"Dolly," Jaffe said, "that's enough."

"... and he was very reassuring. You know, that everything would turn out all right, and that you shouldn't worry, that if it wasn't tomorrow, it would be Sunday morning definitely. He patted me on the knee, right there," she pointed, "as a gesture of reassurance."

"Should he have done that?"

"He did it twice. I guess he must have liked the feel of my knee."

"What else?"

"That's all."

"Are you sure?"

"Well, this one strictly as a value judgment: he seemed like a very autonomous person."

"Stop that, will you please? Just stop that kind of talk."

Dolly's eyes were downcast, as if she was sorry and should have known better.

"Dolly, look me in the eye, will you?" Jaffe watched his wife look up to him. He tried to tune his perceptions to a godlike sensitivity. She fidgeted and looked away. Did that have any meaning? he wondered.

"Hiram," she said, "I'm just not able to understand you today. What do you want me to say? What?"

"Just be honest with me. There's been altogether too much obscurity and deception today. I just want to get one thing straight. Just one."

"Don't be so *sensitive*. Nobody's out to trick you."

"I just want some candor. If not that, then consistency."

"I love you, Hiram. I'm not trying to put one over on you."

"Usually I don't give a damn about candor. But today I want some."

"ALL RIGHT! I opened the door. We recognized each other instantly. Before we could even speak, our clothes were off. He had me in an instant. All the time he smoked his pipe. He even relit it once in the middle. Later, we talked."

Jaffe never flinched. "Didn't Murphy mind?" he asked. "Didn't she show me any loyalty while something like that was going on? No nips at red-beard's ass?"

"Nothing like that happened."

"Simultaneous orgasm?"

"HIRAM, what's the matter? What's the point? It all seems so unnecessary. All I know is I *try* to get through to you. I *try* to relate to your life. I went into ladies' rooms in subways to write down obscenities for you when you were collecting material for that *graffiti* article. I was nearly mugged, raped by girls in leather jackets. But I didn't stop. I wanted to share in your life. That time you were sick I walked the dogs. I met all those nuts you work for. Men exposed themselves in front of me in the park. But I didn't quit. I kept at it so I could share these experiences, share in your life. But I just can't get through to you. You're cold. You're often morose. You're not responsive. You never say you love me."

Jaffe shouted at her. "DIDN'T YOU EVER LEARN TO SPEAK IN ANYTHING BUT CLICHÉS?"

Dolly's eyes were wet and her voice shaking. "That's beside the point. That's not fair. You're trying to change the subject. You're trying to shift the blame on me."

"That's impossible. You're blameless. Everyone knows that. Next to Andrea you're the most blameless, best-adjusted girl in this building, and I don't even know about Andrea anymore, the way she packs a gun."

Her voice came in flooded spasms. "Maybe you love those animals too much. I resent it. All right, it's true.

67

I'm jealous. You've given those dogs some kind of godly traits."

"Come on, Dolly. COME ON. Will you for once stop this totem-and-taboo shit?"

"It's true. You know it's true. It's animal worship. You just don't like to hear it."

"Knock it off, will ya."

"Hiram," she cried, "I love you. I know I do. Why can't you say that to me, say it so I know you mean it? I don't know what to think about us anymore."

The crying got to him, as it usually did. "All right, Dolly," he said softly. "Let's calm down."

"Is it because of this crisis you're having?" she blurted.

"Come on, what's with this *crisis* stuff?"

Lying in bed in a room he never expected to sleep in again, Jaffe thought: life must have some goal other than to move, not just apartments, but up the ladder, into the next bigger office, a new job, another neighborhood, a different town. Is it all just a matter of moving? Look at what it precipitates: you can't think straight while a moving thing happens to you. And what the hell's wrong with standing still? Suppose there was someone like me, who, in his deepest conviction, wasn't really interested in the moving part. Then what?

An hour, at least, and he couldn't find sleep. Parts of his body were moist.

He saw three eight-year-olds on a street corner, an afternoon after school perhaps twenty years ago. One was saying there's a word that if you say it and a policeman hears, they send you to jail. What's the word? he had

68

asked. Kotex, one whispered. It has to do with the army, a secret code word. Japs? Then, as though years and years had never happened, it had come back to him one night in Norfolk when Dolly had told him how awful it was when she got her period at ten: "I had tits when none of my friends did, it made me so self-conscious. For a year I walked around slightly hunched over so nobody would notice." He tried to wrench himself from meaningless memories, but Norfolk was in bed with him. Norfolk: everybody in the world was in the Navy there, yet he was in the Army. Her parents never talked to him as though he could be trusted, preferring the security of their Dolly continuing to date local high school football stars who had gone on to the University of Virginia. Norfolk, a city without cellars. It made lonely young servicemen seduce townies on living room couches. Right under her mother's nose. Her father's nose. He had found it beautiful, the way she felt so enormously confident about that practically public couch. After all, it was her house. But how many football players had lain with her before him on that couch? She confessed to one, but he always believed she might have limited herself numerically out of consideration for his sensitivity. Nor was the couch a question of malice to her parents. They just didn't have cellars in Norfolk, and there was no place in the house. It was too swampy for cellars. Instead of a cellar they had a cavernous two-car garage, a massive thing, big as an airplane hangar, stuffed with lawnmowers and seedbags and pruning shears and buckets and rope and dozens of nearly-empty cans of car polish. And all around Norfolk, wetness and swamp and damp. When Jaffe went up on leave he would think, driving north: sink, Norfolk, sink, thinking it over and over, mile after mile, thinking that if he thought it hard enough the whole place would sink before he returned, just sink, Norfolk, sink.

Her parents' anger when she quit college after a year and went to business school: the way they thought she was pregnant. He finished his tour and went to New York, but still they suspected him. He went to Europe and they forgot him. The way she could type and make those Arabic-looking scrawls, it was good that she could support him for a whole year after they were married.

Were it not for Norfolk, for the dismal, transient, hot, sticky loneliness of Norfolk, would he have married her? The answer seemed obvious: they didn't get married until eight months after he had left Norfolk. That was proof enough. She had given him a feeling of terrible, happy, life-saving beauty in Norfolk, coming along when his existence had reached a low and bleak emptiness. There were others down there before her; he didn't have to marry her. The Virginia Beach schoolteacher crowd, mostly country girls from North Carolina who had come out of the woods, put on shoes, and gone to a teachers' college and taught life's essentials to the children of jaygees and commanders: they were always there, the Virginia Beach schoolteachers, three to five to an apartment—provided, he sometimes felt, for morale and laughs, courtesy of the Bureau of Naval Personnel. How had he lived through the Army in Norfolk? The utter, sleepy desolation of that awful place, that made him at weak moments wish for a war, any war and either side of it, just so he could go and do something, shoot somebody and let it represent

70

whomever he wanted to kill for sticking him down there. Even the sexual odds had been against him, working a night shift in an operations trailer whose long white missiles were ever on the alert for enemy planes that might at any instant penetrate the territorial integrity of the greater Tidewater area. His biggest combat mission came when, in a triumph for the forces of reason, he had talked a drunken duty-Captain out of shooting down an Eastern Airlines plane that had wandered off its flight plan.

Why did all this nourish reverie? It was too apparent: it must be that, like Norfolk, this is the end of one thing and the beginning of something else. To drive off the thought of Norfolk, whose memory seemed to bring on an even heavier flow of perspiration, his mind moved on from that saved airliner to the job he had had—arranged by his brother's connections—writing brochures for another airline three years later. It was then that he had learned of his fear of flying. Twice they had sent him to distant cities and twice he had nearly collapsed from fear in the plane. The way the reports hit the newspapers. Boom—124 dead. Wham—109 dead. An electrical storm—116 dead. And there was never a word about the passengers a week later. Expendable people, they were forgotten that quickly. Fault? It was nobody's fault. A blameless thing, he felt, but who's to say that airplanes aren't involved in a secret, subsidized worldwide euthanasia program? It was no way to die, and if getting from one place to the next meant thinking continuously that he was going to die in a silly, stupid way, it would be best to pass up the airplane thing. A weakness, okay. Admittedly, it may mean that I have some faulty equipment inside, but then so does an air-

71

plane, and that's no good. But look, Dolly said, maybe they'll let you take trains. You said yourself it's such an easy job.

Work for an airline and go around on trains? Impossible. Jobs don't work that way. And it's not just that, it's those people. They're unnerving. The way they speak their own pleasant little language, entirely their own. Every day his boss would come in and chuckle and rub his hands and sit down at his desk and say, "Time for the morning fun and games," and then dive into the correspondence. And the lunches in the cafeteria when all they talked about was their lawns and the pro football games on television and giving up cigarettes. He didn't even smoke, much less own a lawn, or watch football games. Either they were sane and he was mad, or vice versa, he had explained to Dolly. She had called it the crisis of normality and said it was because he had lost touch with common people, spending so much time by himself, writing plays. But he didn't think she really got it. "I will not work with those pleasant zombies." "But you don't have to be one, a pleasant zombie," she'd said. "It's bad even to associate with them," he'd told her. "They're a poisonous orbit."

He would never get to sleep. Is there no way to stop all this from coming back? I'm not a chronic insomniac, but sometimes I really get stuck awake in bed. Why couldn't I have picked some other type of trade? Something that involved hard honest labor, with your hands, the kind of thing that left you fulfilled but knocked out at the end of a day so that sleep came quickly. The effort had been there with him, but rarely the body-tiring hard work that left you sleepy at the end of a day. You've got to work off energy, body energy, not leave it lying around in your head keeping you awake. A carpenter was what he had in mind; a farmer. Or a tree-surgeon. Some old-world craftsman—a meerschaum-carver, say.

A terrible thought flipped him from his right side to his left: what if the superintendent of the new building was in on the attempted burglary? How could he— *Stop it,* he shouted at himself. Just stop it. I get little enough sleep as it is without some baby crying and keeping me up half the night. Then again, if we had a baby and it really left me exhausted I'd be able to sleep when I went to bed and not hang around half the night with all these thoughts. I already know this stuff well enough. Why does it force itself on me? Picker'd have something to say about that. The son of a bitch has something to say about everything. Jaffe always said Picker talked like he had exclusive rights to understanding. Nor did he like Picker's enormous, bushy eyebrows; he exploits his eyebrows every day, he builds his practice around them. For a while Dolly had tried to get him to see Picker, or another psychiatrist of Picker's recommendation. That was a luxury he'd spare himself, Jaffe told her. Or was it an entertainment he'd spare himself? A torture?

Picker had heard enough about his secretary's husband to want to sink his professional teeth into him. He even tried to entice him with a fifty percent discount. Professional courtesy, he called it. "He told me to tell you it's because I'm in the trade," Dolly had said. Jaffe had argued that what he had was a spiritual problem, not a psychiatric one, and that the sooner she understood the difference the better off everyone would be. So far as what your Dr. Picker can treat, I don't have any problems.

Jaffe was positive Dolly had repeated his viewpoint to Picker because the one time he'd met him, when he had picked up Dolly at the office, Picker had told him a story about the French boast that they don't have psychiatric problems like Americans. He said he had once been in Cannes, sitting on a beach and talking to an English newspaperman and his mistress, a French girl in a bikini. The girl had told Picker he must be a very rich American because every American she ever met was going to a psychiatrist. "It's because they're new and their values change with the fashions every couple of years," the girl said. "That's why they have problems. But we French are more confident about ourselves, we don't have such problems, and so we don't need psychiatrists." "But dear," her boyfriend said, "how can you say that? You still wet your bed." The girl snapped at him: "Well, if you don't like it, you can get out!" "And that," said a chortling Dr. Picker, "is the difference between the French and the Americans." He said it in a way that irritated Jaffe beyond measure, so smug and self-assured, as though that one little story explained everything from Sartre and De Gaulle to bidets and berets.

That was the part of Picker that Dolly had picked up, the too-pat explanations, along with the trade jargon which she had mastered pretty well. Dolly could explain away everybody simply by disclosing their early background, their childhood—and feel satisfied she had told everything. She had her own husband pegged by the fact that the toilet training habits of German-Jewish mothers were positively the worst in the world, with obsessive and disagreeable elements of the two cultures combining to wreak maximum havoc upon the children.

Oh Christ, forget about Picker. What's he doing here anyway? He didn't think Picker ever laid a hand on her, although he didn't altogether discount the chance, particularly after Dolly met Picker's wife and described her to Jaffe as a Scarsdale peach.

He tried to wrench himself from his thoughts. They were keeping him agitated inside. Beside him, Dolly slept like a sleeping machine, her breathing annoyingly regular. Jaffe tried to match his breathing to hers, thinking that maybe if he slowed down his respiration rate it would induce a calmer condition inside. He soon began to get out of breath, and the shuddering of the refrigerator motor kept him from concentrating on Dolly's rhythm. At least in our new apartment we won't have to sleep in the same room with a goddam refrigerator, he thought.

Moving would also bring relief from Dolly's incessant reading of the real estate section. She had turned to it the first thing every day for almost a year. It had grown into a hobby. Before even glancing at the headlines, she buried her nose among *Apartments, Manhattan, Unfurnished, three rooms, 80s, 90s*. She knew half the superintendents on the upper West Side. They could have had any number of places while Dolly was at work. Jaffe held out for as long as he could, saying he couldn't be bothered, but finally, inevitably, with superintendents whom his wife had charmed calling to offer them apartments two and three times a week, he gave in.

Dolly told him she was glad that he made the decision,

75

because it meant that now he was ready for the move. Life was so orderly for Dolly, particularly since she had become armed with her trade dialectic. Everything fitted into place. The effort of reading the real estate pages for a year was rewarded with a good apartment at a reasonable rent. Now she could talk to people on the phone, and when she told them they were moving and they'd ask where and what size and how much, and then marvel at the price, Dolly would say: "Well, it wasn't easy. I looked for almost a year. You have to, it's the only way."

What Jaffe wondered was whether Dolly could completely stop reading the real estate pages. Had it become too habitual, ritualistic, for her to give it up? And if she did stop, would she increase the tempo of her antique-store prowling? That was one of her habits that worried Jaffe. He wasn't sure of its application. If, as she said, it was only because Dr. Picker's office was located in the heart of the East Side antique district and it was something for her to do during lunch-time, well, that was okay. But might there be more to it? It could be, as he saw it, an offshoot of her chronic window-shopping. She wasn't a window-shopping addict when he married her; if she was, either he didn't realize it or she concealed it, the latter, tantamount to trickery. And once a year, the culmination of window-shopping came: for her birthday, she'd fly down to Norfolk, and with her mother, would denude the old man's department store of all the copies of things for which she had been building up a long-swelling itch in the New York stores. Sometimes Dolly's tastes worried Jaffe. Her values often revealed a suspicious, provocative side of her that Jaffe didn't trust.

Adolescent mythologies sprayed through his irritated mind. Is it true that English girls like to do it standing up so they don't get pregnant? (Untrue.) That Midwestern girls have big tits because of all the milkshakes they drink? (Unverified, damn it.) Jewish girls are more passionate than non-Jewish girls? (Possibly true, but would need a breakdown as to Orthodox, Conservative, and Reform.)

Maybe it was true, what she hinted at. Maybe he didn't love her. But how could you know a thing like that for sure? How do you know when you are still in love with a person and when you're finished being in love? To get at the answer, isn't it first a question of being honest with yourself? All right, he thought, so let's be honest. His mind went empty for a moment. Nothing came. How do you go about doing that? How do you begin to be honest with yourself? What steps do you take? Let's see, to be honest with yourself, first you've got to . . . and then after that, you should. . . . But the procedure wouldn't reveal itself to him. His mind was collapsing without realizing it. It was nothing you could remember just like that. He tried again. Come on, let's move aside all the dishonest stuff, the clutter, the extraneous, the everyday junk. Let's get down to the essentials, to the honesties. I can get at you. I only need to concentrate a little. Because when I get you, then I can find out about Dolly and me. . . .

But before he could determine (by being honest with himself) whether or not he still loved Dolly, he fell asleep. Nervous exhaustion, Dolly would have called it.

He became the Jaffe of two years ago.

"It was Hiram Jaffe all the way," the man behind the

77

desk was reading aloud, "pitching a one-hitter, batting in the four runs with a grand slam homer." He turned the last page in the scrapbook and came to the back cover which was smudged from when Dolly had spilled fingernail polish on it.

"You were quite the goddamit in high school, huh Jack? But what the hell's a thing like that doing in your scrapbook? You're in the big leagues now. That stuff doesn't count anymore."

Jaffe, irritated by a pimple where his glasses touched the bridge of his nose, felt the bump swell as his cheeks flushed. He was on the job hunt that followed quitting the airline job. But he couldn't even include that experience because he was afraid people would ask too many questions about why he had quit, after working there eight weeks. He seemed to be thinking that on the strength of his clippings and past performances he had gotten nowhere on the job market, and he thought that the notice from his high school newspaper, ten years old and yellow and shredding, might make an impression on someone.

"We're looking for someone to work on the personality end of an account. Client's got the big ego that's gotta be fed."

"Who is the client?" asked Jaffe.

"Jackie Barko Junior," the vice-president answered. He dropped the name with a smirk, pausing, as though he had turned up an ace and was waiting for the full effect to hit home.

"Who's he?"

"Who's he? You kidding? His father was one of the greatest inventors in the world. He invented the alarm clock, for Chrissake. And Barko Junior, you know what he invented?"

"Uh-uh."

"THE BATTERY-POWERED CIGARETTE LIGHTER. What the hell do you think all these goddam lighters are doing all over my desk? They're gifts that I'm gonna give out to the press guys. Look at them. Gold. Engraved, every one of them."

Jaffe picked up a lighter and turned it over. It didn't look like real gold.

"I think it's gold-*plated*."

"What're you, some kind of clown? Listen, this guy says it's gold, it's gold. Jackie Barko Junior's a shrewd cookie. You know what he's doing right now?"

"I guess he's manufacturing cigarette lighters, no?"

"Kids' stuff. Peanuts. He's got some jerk-cousin running the lighter show. Barko is making millions. MILLIONS. He's the money behind the East African meerschaum business. He's mining the stuff like crazy." For a moment, the vice-president went quiet, looking reverent and inspired by the thought. "A guy with the mind for the right gimmick, you know? You can learn something from a brain like that. A guy like him, it's an honor to have him on your client list."

The vice-president pulled the drawer out. "Look at this baby. It's not on the market yet. A battery-powered can-opener. Pretty, huh? Imagine the housewives doing flips when they see this number. You push here, right, and there she goes." It made a quick, whirring sound, although Jaffe didn't see anything moving. "Here you go. Try it. Look at how simple it is. Any jerk can use it."

Jaffe touched it, without meaning to push anything, when suddenly the machine went on, made its whirring noise, and sliced deep into his index finger. With his emotions in such a disorderly state, he didn't even cry out. Instead, he tried to hide the cut, not wanting to make a fool out of himself in front of the vice-president.

"Simple? Here you go, let's have it."

Jaffe leaned forward and handed it back, but in so doing his gouged finger left a rivulet of blood right across the letters on the desk.

"Hey, what the hell're you doing, bleeding all over my desk? What'd you do to your finger?"

"The can opener cut it."

"You covered?"

"Covered?"

"You got major medical? Hospitalization?"

"No, it expired with . . . my last job."

"Jee-*zus*, you can't walk around these days without at least major medical. Your finger's hanging there sort of funny. Go get it fixed."

"I will," said Jaffe. "Don't worry, I'll take care of it. I'm sorry I messed up those papers of yours," he said, motioning to the path of blood across the desk.

"Look, Jack, you got any experience in appliances or home furnishings?"

"No. . . ."

"Chrissake, look at the thing bleed. You're gonna need some stitches. I can't have anyone working for me with a bandaged hand. You don't create a good impression that way. You understand. Right, Jack?"

"I guess I'd better be going."

"No hard feelings?"

"So long," Jaffe said, cradling his hand as he walked out.

There had been a doctor who had fixed him up with five stitches, and the receptionist, as he was leaving, whined sweetly at him in a Bronx accent, "Do you wanna pay for it now, or shall we bill ya?"

"Bill me, bill me."

He must have crammed the day, the way it came back to assault him, because he was on a bus heading downtown. It was a warm February day, so warm that everywhere he looked he saw fur stoles on matrons and the swinging behinds of secretaries who had shed their coats. Everyone looked so fine, in fettle, so confident and glowing that the warm weather had returned at last. Jaffe, on his bus seat, in his bed, wished it was the thick of winter and snowy, the skies gray and the streets slushy.

While waiting at Pot O'Gold Personnel, he watched the switchboard operator, of bottled red hair, holler at a gray-haired man who had his collar button undone: "You'll never get a job that way. Just look at how you look to a prospective employer. You're fifty-five, and these days they ain't banging down the doors for guys your age." The fifty-five-year-old man buttoned his collar and said nothing.

Jaffe was ushered in to see a man who was reading his resumé.

"My name's Gold, Pete Gold," he said, not looking up. "But it's Pot O'Gold, if you want." While he flipped through Jaffe's scrapbook, he took out a chopped egg sandwich which began flaking indiscriminately onto the pages. "Which job did you come to see me about?" he asked, his cheeks swollen with egg and bread.

"The one that said 'bright guy, grow with us, salary open, light account experience.'"

"You're light, I can see that from the scrapbook. In fact, you could be called a lightweight."

"I'm not so bad. It's just that I sliced my finger before," he said, showing him the bandaged hand.

"You got major medical?"

"No. You're the second person who's asked me that today."

"They'll cover you. This is a real good outfit. You gotta be covered today. You never can tell what can happen. Look at *you*."

"I know what you mean."

"Damn right. You're married, right? They give maternity benefits. You gotta know about that stuff. Costs a fortune to have a baby today. You gonna have a baby some day, right?"

Jaffe felt himself stuck for the right answer. He shrugged.

"And they got a profit-sharing deal along with a pension that starts when you're over thirty. It's a sweet company."

"What are they paying?"

"Whatever it is, we get forty percent of the first month's salary, and no screwing around."

"Okay, okay. I'd like to see them, though."

"There's one trouble, though."

"What?"

"They don't take Jews up there."

"But I'm not Jewish," Jaffe lied.

"You're not?"

"No."

"Sounding Jewish is enough with an outfit like that."

"I thought you said it's a sweet company."

"I said sweet, not *liberal.*"

"That's quite true," Jaffe agreed.

"You call me tomorrow and I'll tell you if you got a date with them. Right about now I'm gonna go out and take myself a crap."

Jaffe, wandering, found himself at the Forty-second Street Public Library. On an impulse he must have wandered into the personnel office. A skinny old woman who smelled bad gave him a form to fill out. The thought of filling out another personnel form sickened him, but he filled it out anyway. The woman told him the starting salary was $65 a week, and when he said that was okay, she read his card through, which he had counterfeited with faked jobs to fill in periods when he was writing plays and not working in somebody's office. She gave him suspicious looks. "Can't you do better with a college degree and all this experience?" He didn't seem able to answer her. "There aren't any openings right now, and besides there are a lot of candidates ahead of you," she said.

In the lobby, the library guard made him open his attaché case to see if he had stolen any books, and although he didn't remember stealing any, Jaffe tightened as he watched the guard poke through the various compartments and flaps.

Westward on Forty-second Street toward the subway, past shoeshine boys arguing with policemen, eating a big salted pretzel on the train platform, thinking of how

shabby it must look to have crumbs dropping on your
suit in a train.

"Well, if it isn't Mr. Sick-of-it-all himself." It was Dolly,
sitting on the couch and reading the real estate pages.
"So what's ridiculous today?"

"What?"

"You always come home saying how ridiculous this is
and how ridiculous that is."

"Nothing doing. No more ridiculous than ever."

"So what are you going to do? Kill yourself?"

"Why?"

"Why? Because at least that would change that long
face you've been dragging around here."

The phone rang and he sprang to it. He let the bell
sound two full times because to a prospective employer,
he had been told, it's best not to appear anxious. "Hiram?"
It was his mother. "Creamtop Dairy," he said, disguising
his voice with a Negro accent. A pause. "Oh. . . . I must
have the wrong number." She clicked off and he hung up,
waited, and then the phone rang again, three, four, five,
six rings. She would say *what's new?* and he would start
to squirm because there was nothing to tell her, and she
would start to cry and say, "It's a shame your father never
had his own business. You could have had something to
step right into." It stopped in the middle of the sixth ring.

"Who was that? Why didn't you answer the phone?"

"Wrong number," he said. "Goddam phone company."

"How do you know? You won't pick it up."

"It was my mother. She calls when the weather changes
in February and November. She wants to tell me it's

84

treacherous weather. She's calling to tell me to wear my muffler."

"She is not."

"How would you know? She's my mother."

"Look, what if I was pregnant?"

"I haven't touched you in two months."

"I know, I know. You don't feel so good lately. But if you want to know the truth, I think you're getting a little, on the side. I been thinking of putting a detective agency on your tail."

"I'll give you an agency on your tail in a minute."

"You will? C'mon, I'm ready." She smiled flirtatiously.

"Lemme alone, for Chrissake."

"Well, what if I was."

"Was what?"

"Pregnant. *Enceinte*, pardon my French."

"You know what she says. You can't go bringing kids into the world without having something to step into."

"Like a shoe?" she asked.

They had a major fight. It covered a wide range of grievances, and it started when Jaffe chided Dolly for spending too much time reading real estate ads. He wanted to know what she was thinking of, to read apartment ads when he was out of work. She told him to stop being such a turkey and go collect his unemployment. But to stand in the depressing unemployment offices, in line with all the Negroes and Puerto Ricans, paralyzed him with a super kind of depression. It made him feel like he had sunk to such degrading depths and the two times he had gone, he had nearly fainted from spasms of stomach cramps. It was out of the question to go back, and he felt like a rat for asking why *she* didn't try for a raise in the meantime. Her daddy never let her mother work, she told him, and that was how she was brought up, and she didn't want to work indefinitely. One day she wanted to stop and have babies. "It's like my mother said. You're not trained for anything," she said. "And you're afraid of getting polluted," she added. It bothered Jaffe that she kept looking at his bandaged hand all the time and never once asked what happened.

He was calling Pot O'Gold Personnel, probably the next morning, and a girl told him he had an eleven o'clock appointment at Power, Brower and Peck, Public Relations Consultants. He saw himself dressing, running down the tunnel to the subway, and when he was putting his token in the turnstile, he heard the train rumbling in so he raced down the stairs two steps at a time, feeling very good about flying through the doors just as they were closing. It seemed to give him confidence.

Two stations later, he saw a young man get on the train in a handsome Chesterfield coat. He carried an attaché case and was reading *The Wall Street Journal* with what seemed to be genuine interest and understanding. It was Virgil Trotter, whom Jaffe had known at school eight years ago. Virgil, so polished and professional, looked like he was doing extremely well, it seemed to Jaffe. And then he noticed that the dapper young executive had some kind of dirt mark on his forehead. Jaffe got up from his seat and went to say hello and to tell him about the dirt mark, giving a thought also to the fact that Virgil was a good contact and might have some suggestions for him.

Virgil recognized him, but was not at all polite. After looking Jaffe over and exchanging pleasantries, he returned to reading his *Wall Street Journal*.

"Listen, Virgil, I want to tell you something. You've got a spot on your forehead," Jaffe said. He took his handkerchief and wiped at the mark.

"Are you crazy? It's Ash Wednesday."

"Good God. I didn't know."

"Idiot," Virgil snapped, and he swung his attaché case around, landing a well-aimed blow that caught Jaffe on the side of the head.

Jaffe reeled backwards. The door opened and Virgil strode off. Jaffe clung to a pole, his head spinning, and muttered, "Christians."

It didn't bleed, but it began to swell, almost immediately, and when his station came, Jaffe lingered in front of the mirror on a chewing gum machine. His damaged left temple was bulging and turning purple. Moreover, the tension of recent days was launching a sore on his lip, just as the throbbing nuisance under his eyeglass bridge had been brought to its zenith by accumulating dyspepsia.

He was worried about his appearance. He decided to get a sharp shoeshine at one of the stands on West Forty-second Street, alongside the library. It wouldn't do to give a future employer the impression that he was going to pieces. (Shined shoes can work in my favor; if displayed properly, they could completely steal the show away from the damage to my face and the bandage on my hand.)

He found a Negro shoeshine man who said his name was Andy and would give him a hundred-dollar shine for just twenty cents. That's what I want, Jaffe told himself, the hundred-dollar shine treatment. Andy poured on paste and rubbed in polish with his hand in a way that Jaffe had never seen. Even this lowly shoe-black can take such loving pride in his work that he'll rub it in with his hands and not a brush, Jaffe reflected. It must be satisfying to work with your hands. Before he realized it, Jaffe's shoe was off his foot and Andy was rubbing at it with professional delight.

Suddenly a policeman appeared and said to Andy, "Let's see your license, buddy."

Andy looked up, stunned. "You know I ain't got one. Just lemme finish this shine so I can collect my fare."

"This is the fourth time this morning I've chased you away from this spot. You don't have a license and if you don't disappear fast, you're getting a twenty-five fine."

Andy gathered his shoe box and pulled the folding chair out from under Jaffe. He started retreating.

"Hey," said Jaffe, "let him finish."

"Button your lip, buddy. You saying I don't know my job?" the cop asked him.

"But look, officer, I've got one shoe smudged with polish and he's got the other one." Jaffe raised his one greasy shoe and pointed it at the cop. Then he raised his other foot that just had a sock on it. "What am I supposed to do about that?"

"Shove it," the cop snapped.

"I mean what the hell," Jaffe pleaded.

"Look buddy, I'll book-you-as-an-accessory-in-a-minute."

A crowd had gathered, and into it, ducking and swivel-hipping and pushing, Andy ran out of sight and was lost.

88

"What's it gonna be?" the cop asked, glaring.

"All right, all right. You've succeeded in intimidating me in front of all these people," Jaffe said.

The cop's face brightened. He turned to the crowd. "Okay, folks, move on. He's intimidated."

Jaffe turned and hobbled with his one shoe into the crowd. He looked for Andy, who had the other shoe, but he had disappeared without a trace. There was no sign of him up the street, either.

Jaffe felt panicky. He looked at his watch. It was five minutes to eleven. Inside his pocket he pulled out some change and a few dollar bills: three dollars and forty-two cents. It wasn't enough for a pair of shoes. His bank was uptown in his own neighborhood, and there wasn't time. And Dolly, who worked about twenty blocks away, never carried more than a few dollars with her.

He hobbled to the library steps and put his shod foot up on a step. He polished it to a magnificent gleam with his handkerchief, which still bore a trace of Virgil Trotter's ashes. It looked so good that he decided to go to the interview with just one beautiful shoe and hope that the guy wouldn't notice his other shoe was missing. He limped off toward Madison Avenue.

Because Scott Power, of Power, Brower and Peck, was wearing desert boots, Jaffe felt he was in trouble. He found himself thinking: someone with so much self-confidence that he could get away with wearing desert boots in the office should make mincemeat out of me, in the condition I'm in.

"What's the gimmick behind the one shoe?" Scott Power asked him, his eyes narrowing in studied suspicion.

"No gimmick," Jaffe explained.

"You look like you got ideas," Scott Power smiled. He had an attractively corrupt grin.

Jaffe shrugged and grinned back. "Oh, I don't know...."

"We need a guy with ideas up here. Now look, here's the pitch. We're the PR reps for a New Jersey drug company that's about to capture the attention of the world. They got a scientist over there who's developed a fool-proof, one-hundred-per-cent-positive test for determining if a pregnant woman is carrying a boy or a girl. The rumors have been going around but we're not planning to kick it off really big until next month. Then, *boom*—the works. Column items, a *Life* cover, wire service breaks, science editor junkets, Sunday supplements, a movie deal on the scientist's life, the whole shmear. We even got a guy working on Arnold Toynbee to write a piece on it for the *Times* Magazine Section, just in case anyone's skeptical...."

He looked at Jaffe to measure the effect of his candor. Jaffe massaged his toes because they were sore from the scraping they had taken on the hard pavement.

"Well, don't you care, for God's sake?"

"Certainly," Jaffe said. "That's why I'm here."

"Okay. So as I was telling you, for like two million years women have gotten pregnant and wondered whether it would be a boy or a girl. Now there's no more wondering. This pregnancy test won't leave anything to guesswork. ...Does all this intrigue you?"

Jaffe nodded, and tried to keep a right, three-quarter view facing Scott Power so he wouldn't notice the violent lump on his left temple. It was becoming difficult for him to remember what he had to hide most—his foot, the band-aged hand, or the limp.

"Look what it means in terms of tie-ins. We're going to start a campaign to make future parents sex-conscious months before the baby's born. One of our client's the biggest manufacturer of embroidered bibs in the world. He's already retooling his factories to go into baby clothes because this test bit is going to launch a whole new trend in the production of distinctly male and female baby togs. This guy with the bibs is gonna be a millionaire. Naturally, we got contracts and two-year retainers on account of these tips. Power, Brower and Peck is gonna have the biggest billings in the country in like six months."

Jaffe saw that Scott Power had paused to stare at him. It was probably because he noticed the lumps and bumps and bandages, or maybe because Jaffe was gazing, lost and disbelieving, at Scott Power, wondering which of them was living in the wrong world.

"Our prenatal sales will be tremendous. . . . Do you want to be part of this deal?"

"Yes, yes."

"Okay, now let's get down to brass tacks." He took Jaffe's resumé and scanned it. "Had any training in medical writing?"

"No."

"Worked on any scientific accounts?"

"No."

"In that case, I can't use you on my team right now. You want my advice? Anticipate the greatness of Power, Brower and Peck. Go out and get some baby experience and in a year we'll talk shop."

Jaffe stood up and gave him his hand, which Scott Power shook vigorously. "Good of you to drop in, Jack." With his free hand, Scott Power flipped his resumé into the wastepaper basket.

Jaffe limped quickly down the street to the address of the Career Guidance Consultants. He entered a top management, Georgian-taste office, an American flag spread out over an entire wall. A tall, svelte girl quickly ushered him into a private room with a leather chair and a leather couch. A black-suited man rose from behind a great mahogany desk. Across the man's vest draped a watch chain, and he was so imperial and dignified that Jaffe thought he could be the president of General Motors.

He had difficulty concentrating on what the man said. He didn't even catch his name. He kept thinking about his missing shoe, his finger, the lump on his temple, the coming cold sore on his lip. In a smooth, nasal voice, the imperious man was telling him about America and opportunities—how anyone can make it big. "You mustn't believe the cynics when they tell you about America, and you mustn't leave anything to chance. You simply have to know what your sights are best set on. Then it's a matter of honesty, hard work, and loyalty. That's the key word: loyalty. Know where you're going and be loyal to your goal."

"But how do I know what my goal is?" Jaffe asked him.

"We'll tell you that. Our Career Guidance analysis has served management for a hundred years. We chartered Henry Ford on the right course when he came to us at a young age."

"How much does it cost?"

"Only one thousand dollars."

Jaffe jumped up.

"But look at what an investment it is for your future. We'll *tell* you the answer," the man said, but Jaffe was already out the door and running down the stairs.

In the lobby he fumbled through his pockets for ten cents and called Pot O'Gold. The switchboard put him through.

"Mr. Gold?"

"Pot O'Gold," the voice answered. Jaffe could hear him chewing.

"Has anything come in? Maybe something not too commercial?"

"Who is this?"

"Hiram Jaffe."

"The guy without major medical?"

"Yes, that's right," Jaffe answered, pleased that he had remembered him.

"You covered yet?"

"No."

"What are you waiting for?"

"I'll take care of it, don't worry. Do you have anything?"

"Yeah, maybe I do. I got a foundation, and also an agency with a World's Fair account."

Jaffe wrote down the addresses and phone numbers. He quickly dialed the foundation number, thinking things like: clean—non-commercial—humanitarian—helping people—Guggenheim—Rockefeller.

"CPR."

"Miss Priest?" Jaffe asked.

He was connected and he told Miss Priest, who had a

93

sweet voice, that Pot O'Gold suggested that he call her.

"How nice. Are you interested in our foundation's work, Mr. Jaffe?"

"Very."

"Well, that's wonderful. You see, we here at the Committee for Pigeon Rescue are very short-staffed and you know from reading the newspapers lately what a bad press pigeons have been receiving. All these distorted stories about pigeons carrying diseases in their ka-ka. I think it's just so wonderful that a man should be interested in this type of...."

He hung up. This is the last one, he told himself, absolutely the last. He mopped his perspiring forehead and managed to spread some shoeshine polish on it with his dirty handkerchief. He dialed and made an appointment to see the agency with the World's Fair account. Maybe it's the exhibit with the dinosaurs, he thought, as he hopped down the street. I'd like to fool around with dinosaurs. That could be fun.

There must have been time until the appointment because he found himself killing time, prowling the lonely mid-day lanes of Central Park. Only Jaffe, and women with baby carriages, and the seals. He'd spent so much time there lately that the seals had gotten to know Jaffe personally.

The agency man gave him a sizing-up look. "You a writer?" he asked contemptuously.

"No, not really."

"Look at how you look, all beat up and everything. You look more like a writer than a public relations man. Anybody ever tell you that?"

"No."

"You sure you don't want to be a writer?"

Jaffe shook his head.

"Tell you why I ask. The last account exec we had here wrote plays. One of our clients died and this guy was so busy with some show at a lousy off-Broadway theater that he didn't even get the poor sonofabitch's obit in the morning papers. We caught hell from the client's wife at the funeral. It was a terrible experience. You sure you don't want to be a writer?"

"Honestly, no."

"Okay. Now then. We do publicity for the ninth largest exhibit at the World's Fair. There's a gimmick in the fact that the pavilion also happens to be a nine-sided building. That's because it was built by a Bahai architect. Bahai's got a thing about the number nine." He leaned toward Jaffe and said, "Nine is the biggest whole number before all the others that consist of more than one number. Like ten and eleven. Get it?"

"Yes, I do—"

"Okay. You had any experience with the number nine?"

"Not really what you'd call experience, no."

"Never mind. The pavilion is called 'The Pageant of Do-It-Yourself.' The theme is the land of plenty, where everyone's got enough leisure time to make his own stuff. You know, build your own house, your own boat, hi-fi, furniture. A lot of exhibits like that with guys building stuff. And for the real pros there's a special exhibit—demonstrations on building your own airplane and your own pencil sharpeners. Things that take a little extra manual dexterity. Here, look at this gadget. This baby was assembled from a do-it-yourself kit. A battery-operated can opener. Wanna try it?"

For a moment Jaffe went rigid; then, feeling the pains shoot right through his bandaged finger, he jumped up and bolted for the door.

"You had any hobby-writing experience?" the man called after him.

He was limping down the street, up on one shoe and down on one sock. The sidewalks were jammed with the five-o'clock crowd. He reached the subway entrance and started to jolt down the steps, swept along on the tides of the rush hour. God, he thought, I don't fit into this kind of life. But what kind of life do I fit into?

The suddenness of it shocked him. One second his attaché case containing his scrapbook and resumés was in his hand, and the next second it was ripped out as the citizens of the skyscraper offices bulged forward in a spasmodic knot. It happened so quickly there was no telling whether it was dropped, or wedged in between two bodies, or even jammed up some secretary's dress. At the bottom of the staircase he turned to look up. But he realized this was a mistake because, in stopping, he resisted the currents of people trotting steadily toward the trains. He was thrown to the ground and overrun, becoming engulfed by running feet. He managed to crawl forward and grab onto a woman's coat, pulling himself to an erect position and leaping forward to catch up with the crowd. He struggled to turn around but it was no use. A sudden, driving rush carried him right up to the turnstiles. In went the token and in went Jaffe. He stopped on the other side of the turnstile and turned to look back. "But it's got all

96

my stuff in it, my scrapbook and everything," he heard himself saying. It was impossible to remain standing there, and the only way to move was down the next staircase to the train level. Jaffe closed his eyes and let the crowd carry him along in a steady, packed push.

But going down the steps, someone had stepped on his foot, the one without the shoe. It gave him a terrific shock. He hopped on one foot down the platform and came to rest at a post in front of the newsstand. He stood on his good foot, gingerly holding the right one an inch off the concrete. Glancing around the pole, he looked into the eye of the tunnel and thought he saw the train approaching. A girl's head suddenly leaned out from the other side of a pillar and cut off his vision; she looked right into his face.

Startled, he drew back. She was familiar: the long hair, the brash look. Sure, it was the old neighborhood punchboard. Even in his grief his loins ran hot at the thought of the things they used to do.

"Cherokee, is it really you?"

"Sure, Jaffe, how's it going?" She had that same husky, casual voice, as though for two cents she wouldn't give him the time of the day, but always did.

"It's really wonderful just bumping into you like this. What are you doing with yourself these days?"

"The usual. Hustling a little. What about you?"

"Me? Well, I'm writing, but at the moment I'm kind of in-between, you know—"

"You look like you're having a tough time, kid." She stood there so straight and nonchalant, as if Jaffe wasn't there at all, or as if they had been there a long time together.

"I could never fool you, Cherokee. You're right."

"How about a little fun, kid? Want a fast one to perk you up?"

"Ha, ha. Same old Cherokee."

"I mean this, crumb. She pulled a syringe and a bottle out of her pocket.

"Cherokee!"

The train roared into the station and squealed to a halt. She returned the apparatus to her pocket, shrugged, and without looking at him, said, "Man, did you turn out to be a real nothing. Geronimo, Jack." She walked into the car.

As the train pulled away, Jaffe saw himself standing at the pillar looking down at the tracks. His eyes seemed empty of everything, even irritation. Suddenly he caught himself, appalled at the thought that had entered his mind. "I can't do that, can I?" he said out loud.

There was another train coming into the station, and Jaffe didn't have to look to know how far away it was or how long it would take before it reached him. But coming from behind him he heard shouting, astonished voices, and although he tried to dismiss the sounds, he couldn't help himself and turned around. He saw a little red bird fluttering on top of the pretzel stand.

"First thing I knew, I looked up and there was this bird," said a stout woman carrying a Macy's shopping bag.

"Get him, get him!" a boy yelled, jumping up and reaching for the bird.

"You imagine? A bird down here in the subway. It's like a miracle," said the stout woman.

Jaffe stepped away from the platform and moved to the pretzel stand. He felt a kind of shyness and wonder, and he held up his hand to the bird. For a moment it fluttered almost to the top of his bandage. But then it soared higher and started flying down the platform. Jaffe took off after the bird, shoving his way and running, but not taking his eye off it. He crashed into a man reading the *News* and for a moment lost sight of the bird. The man with the newspaper grabbed hold of him but Jaffe shook himself loose, and smacked the grappling hands down. He flung himself down the platform and saw the red form floating above an up-escalator. He felt wonderfully good, running up the escalator steps after the bird.

He was racing along the street after it, running straight as an arrow, forcing people to get out of his way and causing cars to brake fast when he crossed the street. He had a *glory hallelujah* feeling, tearing up the street after the red bird. Somehow he didn't feel ashamed of being seen on Fifth Avenue with only one shoe and a swollen head and a stitched finger.

He chased the bird clear to Fifty-ninth Street where, blocked by an impenetrable barricade of automobiles, he came to a stop next to a blind Negro man with a German shepherd seeing-eye dog. Jaffe watched the bird sail over the trees into Central Park.

With a secret grin, he pulled off his wristwatch and placed it in the blind man's cup. Next he took off his shoe, which he put in the man's baggy coat pocket. "Do you know Andy, the shoeshine guy?" Jaffe asked.

"Uh-uh."

"Well, he's got the other shoe. You get it from him."

"Thank you, thank you," the blind man said.

Jaffe took out his wallet and placed it close to the dog's mouth, which opened and received it, clamping shut. He watched a moment longer, to make sure the dog held it solidly clasped between his teeth. Jaffe gave the animal a sly wink, and, bending to its furry ear, said, in a voice less than a whisper, "If you see Jaffe, give him his wallet."

Jaffe straightened up and embraced the blind man. Feeling courage, he went on to kiss the sightless eyes. But suddenly there was a flurry at the leash and the dog sprang at him.

The illusion shattered.

He awoke to a jumping commotion in his stomach. Goddamit, he thought in the pitch black, why is all this stuff staging an attack on me? Why now? How do things like that get fixed in your head? I don't still have all those fears, do I? And Dolly isn't like that, is she? For a moment his mind seemed to have gone dull on him: he couldn't remember what had actually happened to him and what was the fantasy. If I live to be a hundred, he asked himself, will I ever know which is the waking part and which is the dreaming part?

FIVE

In the morning he looked particularly bad, an unrested look. His eyes were red-rimmed and the eyeballs themselves seemed unstable, panicky. His whole body felt heavy, achy, and from his right ear there was a beeping of the kind that came only when he'd stayed up the whole night. *How can I feel so terrible? I've been in bed for ten hours.*

Dolly, tugging down the bra she had just snapped on, glanced at him. "What's the matter? Your stomach hurt?"

Jaffe strained to remember his last dream. It had stopped at the point of imminent disaster, seconds ago. Friday night they had loaded everything onto a van and it had all disappeared. There were policemen and they were saying it was stolen, and—no, he couldn't squeeze any more out. It was slipping away fast.

"Here," Dolly said, offering him a capsule. "Try one of these. They're professional samples. They'll settle your stomach."

He closed his eyes at his wife, then opened them. "Settling my stomach will settle nothing," he said.

She shook her hair free after tugging a sweater over her head, and said, "I don't know what's wrong with you, but it shows all over. Why don't you go to a doctor?"

"I have a great spiritual pain."

"I mean it. Why don't you go to a psychiatrist?"

"To have a spiritual pain does not mean you're meat for a psychiatrist. That's what you fail to understand."

Dolly, executing brisk, routine-following little movements, swiped at her hair with a brush four or five times and then bounced up, making quickly for the box that contained their shoes. How, he wondered, could she be so vigorous when he felt so exhausted? "You don't give me credit for understanding anything anymore, do you?" she said.

"That's not so. It's just a case of the less I understand, the more I see that *you* don't understand."

Dolly was going too fast for him. She was making this banter just to fill in the spaces.

"You know what Dr. Picker would say?" Dolly asked, digging through the box. "He'd tell you to stop thinking so much. You're going to wear out your brains. Did you know that after thirty-five men lose thirty-thousand brain cells a day? Those cells only last so long. Look at Murphy. She never thinks. She just lays around. Happy. Silent."

Jaffe eyed the sleeping bulk of his dog, thinking to himself that one day Murphy would jump up and exclaim, "Eureka, I've got it!"

"I'm telling you, Hiram, do you want to know your whole trouble?"

"Even if I don't, you're going to tell me."

"You're too interested in people's motives. You're too critical. Have you ever—is there anyone you've ever just *accepted?* If you could relax and forget about motives and accept people...."

"...I'd make a perfect camel," he broke in, completing the sentence.

"No," she said emphatically, "you wouldn't have to be a camel." Then the doorbell rang and she shouted, "JUST A MINUTE, I DON'T HAVE ANY SHOES ON."

Jaffe sprang out of bed, a blanket pulled around him, and was at the door in two long bounds. "It's them!" he cried to his wife. He pulled open the door.

It was Spiegler, the superintendent, lips firm and eyes gray.

"Mr. Jaffe, you vere supposed to be out yesterday. Vot are you still doing here?"

Jaffe experienced a heartbreaking moment. "Oh, it's you."

"Mr. Jaffe, I vud like an explanation. I haf to verk on dis apartment. Zeh plasterer is supposed to come. All dose holes in zeh vall from your bookshelfs."

"The movers are late. They were supposed to be here yesterday."

"But Mr. Jaffe," Spiegler argued, elaborately opening his hands wide, the gesture implying at once reasonableness, patience, and all their worldly goods out on the sidewalk.

"Look, can I talk to you later? I didn't get much sleep." Jaffe started to ease the door closed.

"Mr. Jaffe, zeh plasterer is supposed to be here in ten, fifteen minutes. Vee must talk about it now."

Jaffe looked down at the floor in a quiet fury that alternated between punching Spiegler in his German-made mouth, slamming the door on him, then simply turning and walking away without even a further word, and mimicking Spiegler, saying *moofuh* for mover.

Spiegler, unaware of the imaginative brutalities to which Jaffe was subjecting him, pushed in another step and surveyed the disarray of boxes. "Here it is Saturday, eleven o'clock. I nefer had such a zing with a tenant. Who is responsible for it?"

"That's a good question, Spiegler, your first good question. The notion of responsibility is—"

Dolly came to the door.

"Ah, Mrs. Jaffe. Good morning," said Spiegler. Jaffe was amazed at the relationship his wife had with the super. The man, in an instant, turned out a handsome smile, complete with a gracious, tilt-headed bow. Jaffe stepped back behind the door and let Dolly take over, which she did, in a babbling, fast voice, full of smiles and apologies. Once she glanced at Jaffe, and found him exposing himself in the direction of the crack in the door, as though to urinate into the hallway on Spiegler's leg. Her expression never wavered, except that her delivery picked up speed, her sorries and perky smiles and irresistible little tricks running into each other. In a minute she was able to close the door quietly on Spiegler.

Without a word, Jaffe walked to the kitchen sink. Standing on his toes, letting the blanket drop from his shoulders, he drilled a loud stream of water into the metal sink, so loud it made him smile.

"Hiram, *stop!* You go too far."

Murphy loped over, gave a puzzled whine, and stood on her hind legs to watch, her front paws resting on the top of the stove.

"Honest to God, that's childish," Dolly insisted.

"The word is vindictive."

"It's insane. I've never seen you do anything like that."

"That's it, let the truth out. You're jealous *you* can't do it. Penis envy. Right? Right?"

Dolly watched a moment longer, and then said, "Oh for heaven's sake, that's *enough*. Didn't you pee all day yesterday?"

She tugged on the high brown boots she had been searching for. They came up almost to her knees. "I'm going to the Greek's for breakfast. Meet me there, okay?"

He glanced at her, not replying.

She stomped past him, "If you ever get finished there."

"Go kick a Jew while you're out," he said, eyeing her massive boots.

"You're crazy," said Dolly, closing the door.

Finished at the sink, Jaffe turned and asked himself why his wife wore those big boots. They make her look like a lady storm-trooper, like a Cossack. And what's feminine about that? It's the goddam fag designers, a whole conspiracy of them. Isn't it amazing what, without sexual power, they can still get women to do? One day all the girls will be walking around with Gupta's toothbrush dangling from their ears if all the fag designers get together and decide that's to be the new fashion. Why don't

105

they do it up right, like they really want? Get them to wear their bras backward, the strap across the tits and cupping the shoulder blades in back. Toothbrushes from the ear-lobes, thigh-high boots, and, yes, maybe a dildo at the crotch this year, instead of wigs and false eyelashes. How do you do, Mrs. Ambassador? What a charming dildo. Is it imported?

He thought he felt like a bath. He felt dirty. But there were three cartons in the bathtub. Besides, since he usually didn't just jump out of bed and have a bath, Dolly would assign it a meaning he didn't care to hear about. The hell with the bath. He opened the medicine chest for his toothbrush and was momentarily surprised to find the shelves empty. Jaffe yelled his wife's name to ask her where she had packed the toothbrushes, then remembered that she had gone out, and wandered back into the living room. Next to the bed he saw an open book, and, on top of it, a note. Maybe that would tell him the location of his toothbrush.

It was in Dolly's handwriting, saying that she was having coffee at the Greek's. She must have been planning to leave without waking me, he thought. The book, a psychosexual paperback she had been reading, was open to a page on which there was a bracketed paragraph that read: "In the inability of the male to satisfy the desire for transcendence by bearing children lies the peculiarly male urge to transcend himself by the creation of man-made things and ideas. The womanly need for children, of transcending the passive role, finds its most natural expression in mother-care and mother-love, in which her creation gives significance and meaning to her life." Jaffe decided to buy his wife a gold star and give it to her for conscientiousness in leaving pertinent passages around for him to read. She left it right underneath the note where he couldn't possibly have failed to read it. Using live ammunition on me at this hour of the morning, he thought.

Rather than giving the book's message any consideration, Jaffe dwelt instead on Dolly's handwriting, going over it for style and meaning. A beautifully slanted script, with graceful, consistent loops that began the ns and rs, it struck Jaffe as pure femininity on paper. Smooth-flowing and terrifyingly level-headed. It was a handwriting that must have earned many an E for Excellence from sixth grade teachers. Somewhere intuitively, Jaffe felt that if a handwriting expert saw Dolly's script and his own messy hand, the expert would surely assert that such a pair were hopelessly mismatched.

His eyes wandered to a box with an unfamiliar notebook sticking out. He tugged it half out and saw that it was his college chemistry notebook, at least twelve, perhaps thirteen years old. Robot-like, Jaffe said aloud to a wall: "He Heaves Little Betsy's Bones Clear North of Florida." Christ, that was it, all right. He still remembered the beginnings of the chemical elements chart: hydrogen, helium, lithium, beryllium, boron, carbon, nitrogen, oxygen, and fluorine. The things he knew, the feats of memory he had performed in his time. For what? So that he could forget everything and be tortured sadistically from outside and within by something like this move, so unrelated to anything he had ever learned? Why had they never taught moving-day in college: the biological, historical, literary, psychological, and philosophical aspects?

He lay stomach-down on the bed and looked from one box to the next. My whole former existence is in these boxes; the secret for the next step is in there somewhere. It only has to be interpreted. He thought: if you go through everything you once learned, the answer should show itself. Don't omit anything. Check the Constitution and dip back into the French Revolution. Maybe glance over the second-grade exercise books. Review the log tables and calculate the value of *pi* to ten decimal places. How long would it take to review everything he had learned (or was supposed to have learned)? Two years? Four years? A lifetime? Conjugate some subjunctive French verbs and get the pluperfect back in shape. Read the *Odyssey*, check out the Old Testament prophets, dip into Shakespeare's tragedies, Ibsen, and Aeschylus. Don't forget the English philosophers from Bacon to Mill. Ditto the Ramayana and the Mahabharata. Read four hundred selected French, Russian, English, and American novels. Check the First Law of Thermodynamics, Plato's *Republic*, the life of Christ, Thucydides' *Peloponnesian War*, *The Canterbury Tales*, Edmund Spencer, Keats, Eliot, and Gerard Manley Hopkins. How much more was there? Get out the zoology book and check into the structure of the cell and the life cycle of the Plasmodium vivax. Hell, really go at it: dissect a frog, and read *The Prophet*.

Jaffe answered the ringing phone almost absent-mindedly, as though too busy with his learning problem for any interruptions.

"It's about time I got you," said a man's voice.

"Who is this?" Jaffe asked.

"Didn't you get my message?"

"What do you mean?"

"I left a message."

"With whom?"

"Look Jaffe, calm down and listen to me. I presume you're kidding when you say you didn't get the message."

"Who should have given me the message?"

Jaffe turned over the piece of paper his wife had left; he wanted to see if it contained further information on the other side. It didn't.

"Who do you think?"

"Is it my wife? Why can't you come right out and say it? Speak directly."

"This is the most direct I can talk. I can't talk any other way."

"Okay. My wife *did* mention last night that perhaps we know each other from someplace. So I guess that's it then, that this is a joke."

There was silence at the other end.

"Hello?" Jaffe called. "Did we get cut off?"

"I'm still here."

"Well," Jaffe said, "is that it? Do we know each other?"

"Perhaps we do."

"Oh for Chrissake, *do* we or *don't* we?"

"It's entirely possible."

"Now look, do you call that being direct? I know *anything* is possible. I deal with possibilities in my own work, but in this case I'm interested in the actual, not possible."

"God only knows what you want me to say to that."

Jaffe thought: is he mad, this mover? Am I mad? How did I get into this? Maybe he's really some kind of crank and I should call the police, although if I did that, and I was wrong, I'd lose his services and then how would I get my stuff moved—the sofa and the piano?

"Look," Jaffe said, "I know you're busy, and I don't want to take up your time. Why can't you just say what it is you called about."

"But I have been saying it. You just haven't been listening."

He's either pretending, Jaffe told himself, or else I've forgotten something important.

"What I wanted to ask you, Jaffe, is the following: does all this writing and not selling get you down?"

"How do you know about that?"

"I know, I know. I also know that you walk dogs for a living, that your wife works for a psychiatrist, that they're building a synagogue across the street from your apartment, that your last play was turned down by more than twenty producers, and that the rent on your new apartment is a hundred and twenty-five dollars a month."

"How do you know all that about me? *How?*"

"What do you mean *how?* I don't understand you. Are these things supposed to be secrets?" The mover gave a short laugh as though Jaffe were the absurd one. "Isn't anyone supposed to know?"

"Well, it's not what I'd call ordinary public knowledge."

"Sure it is. Anybody could find those things out."

"They could not. You've gone to a lot of trouble to find out about me. Why?"

"Why should I?"

"That's what I'm trying to find out."

"Don't be silly. Don't make more problems for yourself."

The thought of someone secretly keeping tabs on him gave Jaffe a twinge of fear. It was ridiculous—and yet there must be some reasonable explanation. Questions raced through his mind: Why has he picked on me? How long has he been snooping into my life? What else does he know? And how does he get his information? What is he after?

Jaffe, deepening his voice, opted for boldness. "Are you trying to up the price for a weekend move? Is that what it is—do you want time-and-a-half?"

The mover laughed. "Do you really take me for an extortionist?"

"That's the only thing that makes sense. That's why you're putting me through the mill, isn't it? I mean, if it's *not* money, then just tell me what in the hell you *do* want."

"Maybe you really don't understand, Jaffe. All right, let me tell you about my business. My business is movement, right? You understand that?"

"Yes."

"Okay. Movement brings me money. Money buys freedom. You've got to earn your freedom because it doesn't just come to you. It's only a freak when someone gets money by not going out after it."

"So?"

"So—that about sums it up. I thought you were supposed to be such a smart guy. You mean you need all the stuff that goes in between? Hell, I've given you a fairer chance than you ever gave me. I don't know why I should be so generous with you."

"How are you being generous with me?"

"By giving you a tip like that."

"You call *that* a tip? Is that your idea of wisdom?"

"Listen, Jaffe, I have accounts to settle. You're one of them. Haven't you understood that much yet?"

"No, not really."

"I think you do. I think you're pretending to be stupid."

"No, I'm telling you, I'm just not getting this too clear."

"Then you should never have started this."

"*Me* start it? *I* didn't start it."

"You originally called *me* about the move, didn't you?"

"Yes, but—" Jaffe stuttered, at a loss for an answer.

"That's starting it. Use a little logic. I have to go now. I'll get back to you this afternoon. I should have some more definite word then, on when we can make it."

The machine clicked and there was the drone in Jaffe's ear. "Goddamit!" he swore. What if I never called this maniac in the first place? Would I have been spared all this? Why, why wasn't I content to sit where I was in the first place? Nothing like this would have happened. Let a sleeping dog lie. Leave well enough alone. Listen to a cliché once in a while, why don't you? They're true, that's why they're clichés.

Now wait a minute, he told himself. This is all such utter nonsense that it's not even worth thinking about. The man has nothing on me. He's just some semiliterate character who can't talk straight and that's what makes for the confusion.

No, he couldn't accept that. How could he not be suspicious now? How could he not help wondering about his probings, the sources of his information? Were he to deny all those suspicions, wouldn't he then turn suspicious of

112

himself for overlooking the obvious? Maybe not. After all, isn't it really a matter of how one takes something like this? You could either take it seriously or dismiss it as trivia. All you have to do is convince yourself that the mover is a prankster—a nuisance and a crank—and it all becomes insignificant. Just the consequences of accidentally choosing some wise guy, something that could have been avoided by picking a responsible mover to begin with. If he could believe that, then he could go on to other things. All right, I'll work on that explanation, he told himself.

But dammit, Jaffe swore to himself, I didn't answer him right. If only they could have that conversation over again. I'd tell him—. Oh hell, what's the use? Stop being such a what-I-should-have-said jerk.

Jaffe suddenly stood up. Murphy looked up at him fearfully, as though she'd just done something wrong. Bitterly, he thought: this goddam moving thing has caused my whole life to pass in front of my eyes, like a man drowning and going down the second time. Possibly the third time.

He glanced down at the pile of boxes around him, and it seemed as if his entire past sprawled there on the floor. Poking out of one box, between the *Aeneid* and the *Odyssey*, which he'd meant to reread but hadn't, was an unfamiliar black shape. He pulled it out: an old wallet, one that he'd used ten years ago. It had a peculiar elliptical bulge pressed onto its surface. He looked inside and to his amazement found an old foil-wrapped Trojan. The way he used to carry one in the wallet, just in case, in high school and college. It gave him a funny feeling, cast him back a decade in a moment. That must have been some kind of landmark in his life, when he stopped carrying rubbers in his wallet. The change must have been gradual; he hadn't noticed it happening.

No, he realized, that wouldn't be the answer, reviewing everything he'd ever learned, or was supposed to learn. That's no solution. For one thing, who would test him and decide how well he had learned? And for another, he could review it all and still not have the answer because the relief he sought might lie somewhere in Byzantine history about which he knew nothing. No, that was too intellectual an approach. There must be another way.

Somewhere outside a truck started up with a great whine.

Jaffe was dressed and wandering around the apartment, pacing. The thought came to him that sometimes he and Dolly could cross the apartment for hours, passing and repassing each other in silence, hostile and unconnected, each occupying the same but different twenty-by-twenty-foot room. Dolly called it periods of emotional privacy, but it worried Jaffe that they could be married and do something like that.

Okay, he told himself, okay. Granted. We'll consider that some other time. Now's the time for action, though. He searched the pockets of his pants. But, having turned out the lining and found nothing, he decided to look elsewhere.

He dialed the number automatically.

"Hello?"

"Hey Oscar? Hiram."

"Hi, kid. You caught me just as I was going out. Got a million things to do today."

Jaffe went right on, pretending he hadn't heard. "Oscar, I'm having a lot of trouble with the movers. They're a day late. I was wondering, if I rented a pick-up truck or something, whether you could help me move my stuff over to the new place."

There was scarcely a moment of deliberation before his brother answered, "I'd love to help you, but I'm having this party tonight. I've got to buy all sorts of crap. Rent some glasses. Get some more booze. The Halloween party."

"Oh . . ."

"Are you coming?"

"I'd forgotten. I didn't know it was a Halloween party."

"Get a costume."

"Isn't it kind of early for Halloween?"

"Yeah, well, I'm going to be out of town next week. The Vegas account."

Jaffe knew there was no point in restating his dilemma. His brother sounded like he wanted to get off the phone quick. It was rare that Oscar ever put himself out past the point of inconvenience. He knew it was the way his brother was constructed and that he couldn't help it, but he was still unable to resist sending some guilt his way. "Okay, Oscar, I was just wondering. I'm in kind of a pickle, and it would only take two hours at the most, for two people. . . ."

"I just can't swing it. Dope it out. There must be another way."

"There is. . . ." Jaffe thought: If I told him I was lying

115

here bleeding, all he'd do would be to give me the number of the nearest hospital.

"Don't forget: get a costume."

"Hey Oscar, one last thing."

"What?"

"Are you really having a Halloween party?"

There was a pause, then in a harried voice, his brother said, "Gotta beat it. Talk to you later."

A Halloween party! What kind of shit is this? Two years ago, in the first year of his brother's marriage, Oscar and his converted wife had given a Passover seder. He had announced it so casually that one would never have suspected that for the previous fifteen years Oscar had never set foot in a synagogue. Passover seder, Halloween party: what's the difference? You do one when you're married and the other when you're divorced.

Jaffe knew that if he were a bigger person he wouldn't have called his brother at all. He must have been hoping for an act of reciprocation. But he was aware he had no right to such an act. Last year, about a month after Oscar and Joan had broken up, he had gotten a frantic call from his brother in the middle of the night. "You've gotta come over here. Someone's gotta stop me from killing myself." Jaffe had dashed over and found his brother lying naked in bed, an empty bottle of scotch on the table and an almost empty bottle of sleeping pills. He never had found out how many pills he had taken, but it couldn't have been too many. He had moaned and cursed, and cursed his parents and cursed the senselessness of his life. Jaffe had listened and nodded and sat passing his brother one cup of coffee after another. Of course it was true, Jaffe knew, that their marriage hadn't had the soundest foundation to begin with. Joan, a cool, tall, long-boned blonde, might have gotten the wrong impression from Oscar's custom-made suits, his sports cars, his floor-to-ceiling wine racks, his park-view $400-a-month penthouse. If she thought his brother was loaded, that was only because of the impression he gave. Before their marriage Oscar had taken magnificent photographs of Joan with his $500 Leica, as pleased with the portrait blow-ups of his beloved as he was with the performance of his telescopic lens. He romanticized and worshipped her beauty and intelligence, as he had done with every girl to whom he had given impossible attributes.

The scene with his brother that night had gone pathetic. Oscar had tramped back over the years to girls Jaffe barely recalled, talking about them as if he had loved them only yesterday, and crying over his loss, throwing blame in a hundred wrong directions. Toward dawn Oscar had turned to his brother, more melodramatic than ever in his onrushing sobriety, and said: "You did the right thing, Hiram. You married a Jewish girl."

"Oh for Chrissake," Jaffe had said, his patience worn out. "That's got nothing to do with anything."

Oscar had stared into the grounds of the coffee cup. "Yes it has. I know it now. I'm being punished for my sins. I went too far."

"Goddammit, Oscar, you can't mean that. You can't reduce it to something that neat. Just who the hell is punishing you, anyway?"

His brother had nodded his head knowingly. "God . . .

destiny . . . nature . . . my father. Whatever you want to call it."

"Shit. Pure shit, Oscar. You and that girl spent two years proving to each other that you were incompatible. Forget about God and destiny."

His brother had persisted. "Even my work is bullshit. I'm ready to throw in the sponge."

"That's a feeling that comes and goes," Jaffe had told him, and, positive his brother wouldn't commit suicide, went home.

It had happened a year ago and Jaffe had wondered about the fact that, compared to his brother, he seemed ridiculously in control of himself. The difference between them, as he had analyzed it, was that Oscar was dishonest with himself and didn't know it, whereas he, Jaffe, wanted to be honest but didn't know how to go about it consistently, thus falling victim to a variety of small and recognizable dishonesties. To Dolly, Jaffe's brother fitted the pathological liar category. Jaffe wasn't sure what that definition consisted of, but he did know that it was intriguing how his brother had all that social charm, how he could be so convincing, how it was possible for someone to talk to him for hours and not realize there was anything wrong with him. "His *problem*," Dolly had urged on Jaffe, "is that he lies." But it was more complex to Jaffe. "Lies is the word *you* use," he had told Dolly. "It's not what he think's *he's* doing, though." When you catch him at a lie, he explained, he seems to be puzzled as to what you're getting at, what this truth thing is that's preferable. He sees the difference between lies and truth as splitting hairs, semantics, sophomorism. It could be that it's an occupational disease of his profession, public relations: the concept *lie* no longer exists for him. It has lost its meaning. Dolly had insisted it was much more personal than that. Jaffe said that when you try to tell him he's not telling the truth he tries to make you feel guilty, like you're making a nuisance of yourself. Instead of truth, he gives you charm and suavity and a sincere-sounding voice. And it works, Jaffe knew, because he had often found himself believing his brother when he knew he shouldn't. In rallying to his brother's defense, Jaffe had taken the position with Dolly, who had become supercritical of Oscar, that his brother's affliction was really caused by an acute shortage of memory. If, as Jaffe had said, Oscar truly couldn't remember what he said from one week to the next, how could he fairly be accused of lies and contradictions? "Blood is thicker than water," Dolly had said to that, adding, "thicker than analysis, too."

Jaffe's new superintendent, who had a gray mustache, was workmanlike in a gray working shirt and gray working pants. He confronted Jaffe in the lobby after he had gone to check his new apartment, which he found in the same condition as it had been last night.

Jaffe said, "I don't think your security here is what it should be."

The super gave his new tenant a sizing-up look. "I heard there was some kind of trouble here last night. Nobody told me what, though."

"It's a security problem."

"This is how it works here: the roof door is locked, the cellar door is locked after four, all the apartments have

peep holes, and the elevator has a mirror. When the doorman leaves his post, he locks the front door. Now if that
isn't good security, I'd like to know what is."

"It's not good enough. For a hundred twenty-five a
month, it's just not good enough."

"Look, Mister Jaffe, there are people living here who
pay twice what you pay. They've got six rooms for two-
fifty a month. And they don't complain."

"They should."

"Why should they? We never have any trouble."

Not completely trusting the new superintendent—because the answer to how the small burglar had gotten
into his apartment last night was not clear to him—Jaffe
said nothing further about the incident.

"Look, I've got to get over to the hardware store to
pick up a few things. Just tell me one thing. Are you
moving in today or not?"

"I can't say."

"If you are, I've got to have a man run the freight
elevator."

"I told you, I can't say."

The superintendent, who dealt in nails and electricity
and plumbing—definite things—stood his ground facing
the new tenant who (he had no way of knowing) dealt
in far less definite things. Jaffe had a feeling that if he
didn't say something, the superintendent would just repeat himself. Was he supposed to slip the man five bucks
to make sure there'd be someone to run the freight elevator? Ten bucks? Jaffe reflected that it was the sort of
problem Oscar would know how to deal with, but his

brother was out getting glasses and booze, and couldn't be reached.

"He's a Jewish gypsy," Dolly's father had told her when she announced she would wed Hiram Jaffe. The pronouncement came back to Jaffe as he walked the upper park path with Murphy—their morning constitutional, Murphy leaving her spoor, and frightening squirrels; Jaffe thinking, thinking, thinking. Her parents had thought they'd seen the last of Jaffe when he left Norfolk. They had breathed their sigh of relief. Free of the army, Jaffe had spent six months in Europe, looking and fornicating, and when he returned to New York he discovered Dolly, by chance, at a party. They called it fate—Dolly's being in New York only for a week-long visit with relatives—and decided to marry.

"We wanted you to have something better," her mother told her.

"I've *got* something better," Dolly answered her. "I've got Hiram."

"He doesn't have a job. He doesn't even know what he's doing with his life."

"I thought a daughter's marriage was supposed to be a happy thing. You're making it sound like a tragedy."

"Dolly," her mother had counseled, "you're very attractive. You could have plenty of nice offers. Why don't you wait? You're trying to build a marriage on sex. It's not enough. There's still time."

"Mother, I *could* have married a Negro."

"WHAT?"

"*Everyone* is marrying Negroes. It's the thing to do."

All this Jaffe knew, and more, because Dolly had relayed the conversations and they had stuck with him for a gloomily long time. At certain times, like this one, they came back. "Are you taking sides with Hiram against us?"

"Mother, it's wrong to say that. I love him, I love him, I love him."

"That's not enough!"

"What's so wrong with Hiram? He does what he wants to do. How many people do that?"

"Drunks, bums, and *goyim,*" her father instructed her.

Jaffe stepped aside to let pass a man and woman with a two-year-old and a pair of new twins jammed into a carriage. The man's feet dragged. Is this scene, Jaffe thought, staged for my benefit? Couldn't they walk somewhere else and not get me all nervous? He felt like going over and asking them why the hell they didn't live in the suburbs.

He watched the quintet recede west. Beyond them the Hudson River ran gray and glassy. It was a day, Jaffe considered, that could go one way or the other.

"What do you want? The wedding or the furniture? You get the presents with the big wedding. Without it, no presents."

Dolly had worked softly on Jaffe for the wedding, he realized afterward, taking advantage of his good nature by saying, "It's really for my parents. Let them have it. It doesn't make any difference to us and it means so much to them."

They had the wedding, a modern classic of squat, unknown people rushing up to an embarrassed Jaffe and shoving envelopes into his hands, envelopes that crackled with the bills and checks inside them. Fathers and uncles danced with four-year-old girls named Judy and Roberta and Lisa and Debbie. There were worried glances when the word circulated that Jaffe didn't dance. Anxious, suspicious, unbelieving eyes, asked, "What do you *mean* he doesn't dance?"

Their wedding, a charade to which Dolly added by managing to look magnificently virginal, was eighty-five hundred dollars' worth of hors d'oeuvres, brassy-band hora music, and sweating, double-breasted aunts. Wasted on Jaffe, it was an affair that set Norfolk Jewry buzzing for months—until the Schwartz extravaganza rumored to cost an even ten thousand, the rumor starting with Mrs. Schwartz. From her mother, Dolly heard Ben had sworn that if he had another daughter, he'd spring for twelve-five gladly. There was a moment, Jaffe knew with his playwright's intuition, a brief moment but a moment nonetheless, when Ben must have thought of adopting a teen-age Jewish waif just so he'd be able to have his revenge on the Schwartzes in a couple of years. Since then, Jaffe knew further, he must have thought that if Dolly divorced her writer, she'd be free to marry again. That, too, would give Ben Korngold the opportunity to regain his place in the community.

Dolly's and Jaffe's parents managed to get along with each other all right, mainly through the sending of cards. They clogged the mails between New York and Norfolk with them, bombarding each other with twenty-five-cent wishes for a Happy Birthday. Happy Anniversary, Get Well Soon, Happy Chanukah, Welcome Back, Happy Mother's Day, Happy Rosh Hashonah. Both mothers—

to them fell the card duties—signed off *Fondly* every single time. Never once *Finally*, or *Foolishly*, *Flippantly*, or *Familiarly*, or *Frantically*. Just *Fondly*. The cards, as Jaffe analyzed it when he took on a job writing free-lance Mother's Day rhymes, served a true and sad purpose: they absolved the senders and the receivers from a legitimate, real closeness.

But then Jaffe also knew it was only a part of the family game. It was also necessary to go through the fiction that there was a normal relationship. He saw the family thing as a Jewish obsession. Formerly their strength and their security in the years of wandering and upheaval, the family was the essence of the faith, the tribal rallying cry. Lie, cheat, wrongdo, anything: but so long as the family is there, the magic bond is intact; there is order amid flux; and Abraham's desert tent is packed full of grateful, loving children.

Under the pretense of normalcy was the formal way he and his father talked to each other, with a queer politeness that was tragic, really, as though they were strangers. There had been so many blowups that now each carried his side of the burden with cool caution. Jaffe's heart, after a session with his father, would vacillate between bitterness and guilt, his father's between frothing torment and silent torment: *aggravation*. With each of them there were things the other could never be forgiven for, deeds done and words said, errors of omission and commission.

Jaffe stopped in a pile of dead brown leaves. He had a moment of insight, when suddenly the reason why all this was returning to him seemed to emerge from the darkness: the past decided, the future held a secret dread—

would the cycle of hostility be repeated, for the sake of justice, between Jaffe and his own son? It was not inevitable, he told himself, and yet there was the fear that what had happened between him and his father could happen to him and his own offspring in a vengeful progression of history that he could avoid only by sheer spermatic restraint. No, there must be ways of raising a child and ways of raising a child. Rule one: leave him alone about religion and raise him as a pagan, and if he finds religion, let it be as an adult and not forced on him at nine or ten. Rule two: talk to him about important matters and avoid passivity. Rule three: expect no gratitude, and strike the word *deserve* from the dictionary. Rule four: parents owe children everything; children owe parents nothing. Rule five: parents should imitate birds and find happiness in seeing their young fly away.

All the rest, from the toilet training to the expectations of success, would take care of itself. Because it didn't seem terribly complicated to Jaffe, he felt the usual hidden distrust—his inadequacy—that there must obviously be a good deal more he didn't know about.

"Hey, hey you."

A woman's voice drove the thought out of Jaffe's mind. He turned and saw a portly shape, somewhat disorderly, bearing down on him. He walked faster. He didn't feel like any new surprises.

But there was Hobbs, in front of him, sitting imperially atop his charger. Oh for Chrissake, thought Jaffe, stopping.

The woman waddled up to him.

"How could you do that? How could you? Can't you show a little common courtesy?"

Jaffe stared at her. He'd never seen her before in his life.

"That's mine up there," she said pointing. "The black and white one."

On the slope above them, a near-Dalmatian was humping Murphy, who stood looking down at Jaffe, oblivious to the commotion on her hindquarters.

"He's been following her for the last twenty minutes. I've been calling. Didn't you hear?"

"No, I was thinking."

"I'm running and hollering. He don't come back so good. She in heat?"

"No."

"Wheeeoi," the woman exhaled, putting a hand on her chest. "I don't have such a good heart. The doctor said walking would be good but he didn't say anything about running.... You sure she's not in heat?"

"Positive."

"Jaffe...."

"Hobbs...."

The mounted cop was pointing at Murphy. "Where are the rest of them?"

"It's Saturday. My clients are home from work and they take their own dogs out."

"You mean it's for your own pleasure, not even business? And *still* the dog is off the leash?"

"Fantastic, isn't it, Hobbie?"

"Jaffe, how long are you going to flaunt the law?"

"Look, Hobbs, get off your goddam horse, take off your

126

goddam badge, and let's go behind the tree and settle this, man to man. After you've beaten my brains out maybe you won't bother me anymore about the dogs. Okay?"

"OH!" the woman cried, backing off with her white and black dog.

Hobbs made a small head-shaking gesture, as though in pity for the young citizen before him. He observed a clever look brightening on the face before him, and the dog-walker took a step closer to him. As if to keep Jaffe at a distance, Hobbs made a crashing noise in his throat and spit into a pile of leaves.

"Hobbsie, I just had an idea. What are your plans after work? What do you do with your off-duty time?"

The policeman sat tall, saying nothing.

"Maybe we could make a deal, Hobbsie. . . ."

"Careful, Jaffe. I don't like the sound of this."

Jaffe whispered. "Loitering for the purposes of solicitation. Public indecencies. Prostitution."

"Huh?"

"Buggery in the bushes," Jaffe whispered.

"What the hell are you talking about?"

"Right on your own beat."

"I still don't—"

"Hobbs, I'm giving you a tip. I thought cops loved to get tips."

"Yeah, but . . ."

"All these perverts and deviates you're always looking for—they're out here at night. All over the place. They're screwing each other in the bushes. They're dressed as women. They're soliciting from passing cars. I'm talking about male prostitution."

Hobbs seemed interested. "Here?"

"Every night. On the beat that you take such good care of during the day. At night it's a cesspool of sin. No decent citizen can walk—"

Hobbs stopped posing on his horse for a moment, in an effort to think it over.

"Jaffe, is this true?"

"A deal's a deal, Hobbs. You get yourself a little night duty. Put in some overtime and come down here and see for yourself. And when you get them, Hobbs, and you get yourself a citation, just remember who gave you the tip. That's all I ask. If you get them, you leave me alone with my dogs. Fair?"

Jaffe turned and walked slowly off with the still un-leashed Murphy, feeling the real physical presence of the policeman's narrowed eyes on his back.

Jaffe's phone was ringing, and it continued to ring as he ran up the stairs, and it rang while he twisted the key into the lock. As he ran swivel-hipping through the boxes it stopped ringing.

Where the hell was Dolly? Why wasn't she here?

Then the phone came to life under his hand.

"Jaffe, you still there?"

"Of course I am. I'm waiting for you. Where would you expect me to be?"

"You didn't answer when I called before."

"I was out. I just came back. I can't stay in this chaotic apartment every minute. You're twenty-four hours late

128

now, and this place is okay when things are in place but it's all piled up and in boxes—it's not easy to take."

"I know, that's a natural reaction."

Jaffe cursed himself: he'd take anything from this mover, because he wanted him to do the move. He was annoyed at his own cowardice for not just hanging up and telling the man to go to hell. If he did that, he knew, he'd have to come up with some other way to move, and on the weekend how could he do that? Better, he felt, to put up with this character and play the game his way.

"Jaffe, do you ever compare yourself to me?"

"What? How can I? I don't even know you."

"You're still sticking to that line, eh? Okay, that's your privilege."

"It's not a question of privilege. It's—"

"But when I compare myself to *you,* I know I've been places you've never glimpsed. And the joke of it is that you call yourself an artist. I don't make that claim, but I'm sure if I decided to be an artist, I could draw on the things I've seen that you've never even glimpsed. You're lucky you don't have guys like me to compete with. You're lucky I'm in a different business."

"Art isn't a business."

"That's what *you* say. I know different."

"So what? So what if it is?"

"You're getting away with murder, that's the point. Here, I'll throw a little scare into you: I'm just now dabbling with sculpture. My first attempt, comparatively, outdistances anything you can do in your medium."

"So?"

"So? Look Jaffe, your trouble is that because you never

work hard enough, you worry about things that aren't your concern."

"Jesus Christ! All right, assuming you're right, what does it prove? Why tell me all this?"

"Just food for thought. Something to mull over. So you won't get too satisfied with yourself. You'll see what I mean."

"You're talking in riddles."

"I'm talking perfectly straight. You're just not understanding. That's always been your problem."

"For heaven's sake, I'm trying to follow you. But all this talk doesn't seem to lead anywhere. It doesn't get you over here or get my furniture moved."

"You expect too much."

"What do you mean? You're the mover. God only knows what you want from me."

"Maybe He does and maybe He doesn't."

Jaffe wondered: what does this bastard have on me? Have I forgotten that I once did something to him that I shouldn't have? After all, you can't remember everything.

"Jaffe, I want to tell you something. You have to succeed by your own efforts."

Jaffe swallowed. "I already know that."

"Don't depend on anyone. A group, a company, your family."

"I don't."

"*Of course you do.* Don't be so damned agreeable with me. Everyone depends a little. In order to get by, people have to perform little services for each other. Somebody's grown and packaged and stored all the food you eat.

Somebody's made the clothes you wear. That's depending, isn't it? Even the so-called independent types. An artist paints a picture. Someone has to pay him for it, right? Otherwise, no more paints or canvas, and he doesn't paint."

"So?" Jaffe was thinking how strangely naive all this sounded.

"Here's the point. I'm getting out of the moving business. I won't have to depend on people like you anymore."

"I wasn't aware you ever depended on me. I thought I was depending on *you.* "

"I'm getting out of the moving business *and* I'm going into the wrecking and junk business. I've looked over the field and I've decided that in America, in this period, that's where the money's to be made. That's where you can eventually find the greatest amount of freedom. It's the time of tearing down and throwing up. There's more tearing down going on than ever before. We worship new things, so we tear down in order to put up the new. That's where I come into the picture—the tearer. I'll tear down buildings of all kinds—office buildings, apartment buildings, hotels, public places. There's absolutely no waste. Once you've got it all torn down, the girders and bricks and windows, you sell the junk to someone else who polishes it up and resells it. Absolutely no waste. Next year at this time I plan to be rich—and free."

"That's not the way it works," Jaffe protested. "It can't be that simple."

"It is! It is just *that* simple. Period."

"All right, all right. If you say so. When are you going into your new business?"

"Yours is my last move. I start wrecking Monday."

Why me? Jaffe kept asking himself. How does he get to me?

"I'm still comparing, Jaffe. And a major difference between us is that I made it by muscle. I washed dishes in college and played on the football team. I was in the infantry in the army, and I lugged stuff around after. When you're making it by muscle, you have no choice."

"But originally you had a choice between making it by muscle and making it some other way. You chose muscle. That's a choice."

"No, that's an illusion. Making it by muscle comes from how you're born. I came onto the scene with these terrific shoulders and arms and before I was old enough to exercise a proper choice I was getting shoved into things as a result of my muscles. People came to expect me to do certain things. And after a while even *I* assumed that was my real nature."

"But maybe it really is."

"Don't go pulling your Jewish superiority on me."

"What do you mean? I'm just talking to you." He heard a burst of disgust blown through the mover's nose.

"You just can't see me having any *yikhus*, can you?"

"What do you know about *yikhus*?"

"You see? Just from the sound of your voice, you give yourself away. You think that because I lug stuff around I don't read, that I've got no mind, that I don't know about culture and books. That's typical of you."

Jaffe thought a moment, wondering, is this it? Some anti-Semitic thing in back of it?

132

"I'm perfectly aware that you've got a mind. It's just that I don't know how it works, that's all."

"My wife recognized your name, Jaffe. She saw your plays a few years ago when she was in on a trip from California. They impressed her."

"No kidding!"

"When she heard your name again, she mentioned it to me, and she started this whole bit about how you must be a big, famous playwright by now. Believe me, she was pretty surprised to learn that you live in a crappy, one-room studio. But you started the ball rolling with her. All of a sudden she wants more culture in her life. She even said how it must be fascinating to live with a writer. And she didn't just say writer, she said *dramatist*, with a long, drawn-out *a*."

Could this be the logic behind everything? Now, recalling other fragments of their conversation, Jaffe devised a perfectly logical question to ask the mover. But another question remained: was it safe to ask? Why don't you ask him? Jaffe coaxed himself. "Why don't you quit the monkey business and just move me?" he was on the verge of asking, but he withheld the question, fearing the answer. Because somewhere he had once read that an answer is a form of death.

"I used to be a bum," the mover was saying in what Jaffe nervously felt was a new, confessional sort of voice. "I went through a long bum stage. I didn't work. I lived off people. Drank. Smoked pot. But I decided I didn't want to get used to pain and hardship. It makes you callous. You lose your capacity for fine human feelings. I'm no bum anymore, Jaffe."

There was a pause and Jaffe threw in, "You don't even talk like one."

"Nor do I act like one. I'm industrious, and steady as a stone."

"You're even self-righteous about it."

"That kind of talk is going to get you in trouble."

Jaffe was at a loss for an answer.

"For a time I went way backwards. I thought about committing suicide. I raved and I floated. I couldn't get my feet on the ground. I was a drifter doing odd jobs, picking grapes, loading trucks at the docks, waiting on tables. Shit work. People would look at a guy like me and think, 'Hell, this guy's used to it. He doesn't feel anything.' I slept on beaches and on other people's floors. I nested with Commies and nymphos and fags and religious fanatics, all of them dirty and full of talk. But I've renounced all that. I wasted an awful lot of time and I'm making up for it now. I am my own liberator, do you understand?"

Jaffe didn't want him to go on. He didn't want to hear any more because of a sudden fear that the mover must require something of Jaffe in return for spilling his secrets. He experienced a moment of dizziness, thinking: it's gone way past a game. It's now at the point where it can lead to all kinds of danger. Jaffe could actually feel the color draining from his face.

"Myrna was my anchor in space. She brought me back to reality. She's gorgeous. You ought to see her. She's a Catholic girl."

"Don't tell me any more. I don't want to hear any more."

"Jaffe, if you don't listen to good advice, you'll have to learn by bitter experience."

"But that's always been the case with me."

"For me, Myrna was—"

"No. I don't want to hear any more. I don't want to listen."

"Then you'd better hang up."

Jaffe did just that, and discovered that his body was wet with perspiration. God, he thought, I'd do anything to be finished with this moving.

His heart slowed its speeding beat, and, more in control, he thought: am I afraid of him? Can he hurt me? He's probably powerful—he's a mover. Dolly said he had muscles. But that's not how he can hurt me. It's the internal damage he's doing.

Maybe he's insane. But then, was the man at the phone company also insane? And, for that matter, the people at the airline where he worked? And the lady with the black and white dog? His in-laws? Hobbs? That's dangerous, Jaffe thought, because at one time or another he'd thought them all mad. And he knew that couldn't be.

All right, say he's not insane. Then I'll play his game. I'll stick around the phone. NO! The hell with him. Make it Sunday. I'll leave a note downstairs at the mailbox in case he comes.

Sonofabitch, Jaffe thought, shooing Murphy out the front door, you just never knew where you stood with this bastard mover.

Distressed that he didn't know where Dolly had gone, and unable to face the chaos of his possessions in the apartment, Jaffe returned to the park with Murphy. He went back into the brush and trees of nature because he didn't think he could take any more trouble—from the telephone, the mover, Spiegler.

Damaging thoughts insinuated themselves into his mind. It's nothing more than a common misunderstanding, a run-of-the-mill sort of thing, isn't it? He found a confirming nod. It's really all in my head, interpreting unnecessarily. I made a mistake and hired an irresponsible mover. And they've got a smart guy at the phone company having a nervous breakdown, and the painter is a victim of, say, urban stress. The burglar, too. They're all accidents, no more connected than ... but he broke off. He was lecturing himself so unconvincingly that he had to stop. If I didn't know better, he mused, I'd swear someone was playing some kind of trick on me.

Is there any possibility of calling off the entire move? It had become such a painful process—the transplantation. And, after all, he had learned his lesson. Stay where you are. That's what the Jews knew during the war. All hell was closing in on them, he thought in a flash of insight, but they rejected the further hell of moving themselves and all their things. The Jews knew. They stood their ground, stayed where they were, paralyzed by the fear of moving, and got slaughtered. No, any good historian would make mincemeat out of that. And yet—

But how can I stop it? The machinery is in motion. I can't just stay in the old apartment and unpack the boxes, hang the curtains up again. There are new tenants coming in; a lease has been signed, and whoever the new tenants are, they've made their own arrangements to vacate an old apartment, too, for which another has signed up; and beyond that, others, ad infinitum—a complex, interlocking

136

arrangement of movers-out and movers-in, new leases and vacated space, trunks and boxes stretching back and controlling a dozen people, two dozen, a hundred, even. And it all depended on Jaffe. He couldn't just stop the process. It would be inhuman.

Cutting off the path and stepping into the woods, he recalled Zoroastrianism's sixth commandment: thou shalt plant trees and breed cattle. There's a commandment for you, not like the phony, unreasonable ten where the game now is to break them as fast and as often as possible. All I want is that I shouldn't have to lie and contrive, he reflected; and the kind of honesty I seek could come, conceivably, from planting trees and breeding cattle. Could it be that it's all connected with making it by muscle, and that's what the mover was trying to tell me? But how am I ever going to get anywhere when I've never caught my own dinner, never shot a deer, felled a pheasant, caught a fish, or gone clamming? All my food has always come from stores, he thought sadly.

He sat down under a tree, the leaves a little moist under his bottom. And with Dolly bent on populating our new apartment, it's not going to get easier. Let's be realistic about that thing. Becoming a mother might be *her* way out, but what about mine? A mother's not a girl any more —a lover. She's a diaper-washer, housecleaner, naggerafter-kids, a yeller, a pediatrician-caller.

Dammit, he thought, I'd feel better if Dolly was home to take messages. It was difficult for him to pinpoint the apprehension he felt. Somehow it all went together: the move, his problems with Dolly, the way he was trying to wrench himself from his memories of endless madness,

137

past and present, that had suddenly tumbled in on him. And this mover: what is he? What does he have on me? Is he warning me? Maybe. But what is he warning me about? And why do I submit to him so meekly? (A dimmer voice, which he didn't like, answered that it wasn't only Jaffe in the picture, that there were two of them, he and Dolly, and since he was in charge, having duties to fulfill as a husband and head-of-the-family, he had to be cautious.) I've been more compliant toward him than I've been toward anyone in a long time. But then, he gives me no choice. I can either buck him completely or just be compliant. And in choosing the latter, I seem to run the danger of becoming his . . . his what? Sounding board? Slave? Scapegoat?

Maybe I should try listening to him more carefully. Perhaps it's a mistake to assume that I shouldn't take him seriously, that I shouldn't take his words at face value. But if I did take him seriously, then what?

Here's what I want to know about this move: specifically, specifically and exactly, what am I moving from, and to, and why?

SIX

"Excuse me, do you know anything about electricity?"

"What?" The girl's voice collapsed his daydreams.

"I mean, are you handy?"

She had on tight, tight jeans. Yellow hair fell straight onto her shoulders, hair that fluttered like corn silk. Her oversized, turtle-neck sweater (maroon) gave her a casual, sloppy look, nonetheless feminine. She had a young, kindred face, her mouth perhaps a little too wide, but still kindred and open.

"Did I wake you?"

"No, no," he protested, suddenly embarrassed. "I was just thinking."

"Actually, I saw your dog first."

Jaffe nodded.

"That one's mine over there." She pointed.

"A liver-and-white springer!"

"Freckles."

"That's a good name. . . . Female?"

"Male."

Jaffe let his eyes roam her face, almost as if his hand were doing it, caressing her. What a pretty girl. That hair. No make-up.

He said, "I've never seen you down here before. Did you just get your dog?"

"No, but I sleep late. I usually come out around ten o'clock."

"I'm in by then."

"I've seen you, though. You usually have five or six dogs with you. You're the guy with the service, right?"

"Right."

She had squatted on her haunches, three feet from Jaffe, and was stroking Murphy's great head. Murphy's eyes rolled back in ecstasy.

"The stuff in my refrigerator is going to spoil."

"Oh, the electricity. You've got no electricity?"

She nodded. "It's a brownstone and the janitor's never around on weekends."

"Maybe it's just a fuse."

She shrugged. "Just! I still wouldn't know what to do."

"I'd be happy to take a look. We'll buy some fuses on the way back." Jaffe said it before the words were considered. They just tumbled out.

"But I don't have any money with me. I couldn't let you pay for my fuses."

They glanced into each other's eyes, then glanced away.

"Pay me back later," Jaffe said.

Her apartment was dark as a bat's cave. "But why don't you open the window shutters?" Jaffe asked.

"Because I'm on the first floor and I don't like people looking in here."

"But just till I check the fuse. So I can have some light."

"No."

She consented to striking a match, and Jaffe searched the upper limits of her walls until he found the box.

"Here we go," he said, pulling over a chair, and leaping up on it. The chair wobbled jerkily and Jaffe clawed at the wall.

"Don't you have anything steadier?"

"That's the steadiest."

"If I fall, you'll have to give me first aid in the dark. Can you do that?"

Jaffe heard her giggle.

"I better hold your legs," she said, adding, "because I don't know anything about first aid. It's a Salvation Army chair."

Jaffe struck a new match at the fuse box, and pulled back the cover. As he unscrewed the old fuses, he thought: how strange—ten minutes ago I was sitting in silence in the park and now, through what magic do I stand here on a ladder, looking in a fuse box, an unknown girl's hands on my legs?

There was a whine from below him: Murphy's worried query as she observed her master looming up at a frightening height. The girl's dog had his nose buried someplace in Murphy's rear-end fur, his stubby tail switching to and fro.

A small lamp popped on, and the refrigerator motor groaned.

"You *did* it!" she cried.

141

"Magic," Jaffe said, stepping down off the chair.

"You handled that in a very masculine way," she said.

"I know I did."

"Can I reward you with a cup of coffee?"

Her question seemed to turn on a switch in his stomach.

"Hey, suddenly I'm hungry. I didn't eat breakfast, but until now I didn't notice it. Until this moment I didn't have any appetite."

"How come you didn't have any breakfast?"

"Because I'm moving today and everything has been very uncertain since the movers are late, and my stuff is all packed, the coffee pot and everything. I just didn't feel like eating anything, I guess."

"Sit down there." She pointed to a small table. "I'll fix something."

The apartment, with just one light on, remained practically dark. He could see clothes and books strewn on the daybed behind him, and in the opposite corner a suitcase, rucksack, and four picture frames embraced each other in a heap. A tattered Mexican rug hung on one wall, a great brown stain (coffee or wine? Jaffe wondered) on the upper right-hand corner. The room had a sloppy, junk-heap, lived-in look. Nothing had a permanent place, at least not that a single forty-watt bulb could reveal. With the corners unlit, and the shutters hiding the outside, the place seemed excitingly remote—secretive, even.

The girl had taken off her sweater. Under it she wore a white mesh jersey, the kind they wear at the beach, Jaffe thought. Her arms seemed to shine orange.

"How is it you have such a terrific suntan? It's October."

"I came in from California last month. I spent a lot of time by the sea this summer. This is nothing," she said, looking down at her left arm. "You should have seen me in July."

"That's really some color—for a blonde."

"That's what everybody says: 'For a blonde.'"

The butter sizzled in the pan. Jaffe noticed she had a gold chain around her neck and wondered what was at the end of it. He watched her bend over.

"Freckles!" she said sternly, pushing at the dog who refused to cease molesting Murphy. The chain had slipped out of her jersey, and Jaffe saw a cross at the end of it. "I better put him in the bathroom before he comes all over the place."

Jaffe thought that was an odd thing to say, and out of the silence following her remark, which seemed to linger heavily, he found himself telling a dog story, observing that he had known an old woman in the park the year before who carried a little toy terrier around with her. She used to chew the food first, take it out of her mouth and then give it to the dog. "It was one of the most compassionate things I've ever seen."

"Why?" the girl asked. "Why did she do that?"

"The dog's teeth were shot. It was quite old."

She turned off the flame under the eggs. "You're right. That is compassionate."

"And I'll tell you something else about that woman."

"What?"

"She didn't always chew her dog's food first. She used to do other things with her life."

"She sounds like a recluse."

"She was."

She sighed. "Sometimes I think that's what I'll be some day."

"You?"

She gave a quick up-and-down nod.

"That's ridiculous," Jaffe said.

"Here are your eggs."

The girl pulled up a chair next to him and placed her elbow on the table, her chin in her hand, and watched him eat.

"Why a recluse?" Jaffe asked.

"Because one of these days I'm going to be sick and tired of having people look at me. I feel sure of it." She sat up and arched her back, forcing her chest forward so that her breasts sat over the edge of the table, practically in Jaffe's bread plate.

"I see what you mean," Jaffe noted.

She let out an impish little laugh and sat back, replacing her elbow on the table, chin in hand. She seemed to wear permanently a playful, mirthful little smile that went well with her tousled blonde hair and orange-red cheeks. Her face was so young, so fresh, Jaffe thought. What little light there was in the room seemed to shine on her cheeks. There was something young and animal-like about her, irresistible to Jaffe—the way she had holed up in this dark, sloppy little place.

"What do you do? You said you don't go out till ten in the morning."

"Modeling. Some TV work. A little acting. I came in for a bunch of commercials. That's what I meant about people watching me."

144

With every bite, Jaffe could feel her eyes following his fork from the plate to his mouth.

"Then this isn't your apartment."

"A friend's. She's in Europe. I usually stay with her when I'm in New York. She stays with me when she comes to California."

She sat upright, on what appeared to be a whim, and then slouched back down in the chair. She was still looking at him intensely, but no longer in such a concentrated, clinical way.

"You passed," she said. "Flying colors."

"What do you mean?"

"I can tell a lot about people from the way they eat their sunny-side eggs. It rarely fails."

"How?"

She started chewing on her gold chain as Jaffe drank his coffee. "First you worked on the edges, the white stuff. You were very careful not to disturb the yolk. The last thing you did, you popped the whole yolk into your mouth so you wouldn't have to break it. That's the kind of man I like. It means you're sensitive and gentle."

"What if I'd have cut into the yolk at the end and let it ooze out?"

Instead of an answer she nodded her head, as though the conclusion must be self-evident.

"That's a very instinctive approach to human behavior," Jaffe said, and he couldn't fail to think how different it was from Dolly with her Freudian vocabulary. Still, he fought back the thought, pushing aside not only comparisons but the thought of Dolly altogether.

"My late husband was a real butcher with fried eggs.

145

First thing he did was break the yolk with his fork and spread it out all over the white part."

"Does that mean you weren't happily married?"

"He wanted to play musical chairs all the time. You know—"

"What do you mean? He was crazy?"

"No. Musical chairs. Musical wives. It's a California expression. It's the big game with these Navy fliers. Screwing your way through the squadron's wives. All they do is fly and swap wives."

"Hey, no kidding," said Jaffe.

"Whenever you see them on television, those pilot guys, they all look so clean-cut, like they could advertise kid's cereals. But they're really just kids themselves, and boffing a different buddy's wife every week is all part of the whole flying game."

"No kidding," Jaffe said again, astonished that military men would have the imagination for that.

"Sure."

"So what happened?"

"A week after I left him he missed the carrier he was landing on. That was it."

"That's not a nice way to die."

"Better off. If he was still alive he'd be over there charcoaling almond-eyed kids and loving the whole shooting and flying game. At least I know he had no part in that."

"Does that mean you're some kind of activist?"

"I'm an activist, a pacifist, a sensualist—and I surf. I'm an all-California kid."

"But why did you marry him? You're smart and he sounds so shallow."

146

"Why? He was the handsomest son of a bitch you ever saw. Sort of a dark blonde complexion and a big grin with white teeth. He was handsomer than any movie guy that every played a Navy pilot. I still go drippy when I see some handsome guy in a uniform."

"Isn't that strange," Jaffe commented rhetorically. From her expression, he could see she was still thinking of her late husband.

"Why strange?"

"Why? Well, you sound like you didn't like him, and yet—"

She shrugged. "It's possible to love someone but not to like him. I loved him, but I didn't *like* him."

Jaffe repeated the thought to himself, and said, "That's okay. Mind if I use that sometime?"

She didn't answer at first, but then said, "Why do you keep staring at my chain?"

"It looks out of place on you."

"I wear it because I have a great many fears. It helps a little."

"I have fears, too," Jaffe sympathized.

"What's your dominant fear?"

"Mine?" Jaffe asked. "Well, I have certain *apprehensions*. I don't know whether they're classified as fears. I'd say I have a great fear of wasting my life."

"One of my big fears concerns my late husband. He ruined it for me, the bastard. He had the biggest thing of any man I ever slept with. It was always an anticlimax after him."

Jaffe snorted. "That's not a fear. That's a typically

147

American outlook. Thinking like that leads to nothing but supermarkets and Cadillacs."

"What do you mean?"

"Bigness, not quality. Let me tell you what a Negro lady cook once told me in a Catskill hotel where I worked. She said, 'Although a man may not be able to touch bottom he can still do hell around the sides.' It's from the Chinese."

"Did you sleep with her?"

"The cook?"

"Yes."

"No, but I studied with her that summer."

She got up and walked behind Jaffe to the forty-watt bulb. She clicked it off. Jaffe turned around but couldn't see her in the darkened room. A snap sounded, followed by a zipper's noise. "All right, my Chinese lover. Come revise my viewpoint."

Jaffe groped toward her. They fumbled for a moment with each other's clothes. Then he moved down onto her.

"Ouch," she squealed, "what are you trying to do? Bite my titties off?"

He was thinking wondrously, in the calm that followed, of something Oscar had told him a long time ago, when sex to Jaffe was as mysterious as driving a car. "They're all alike in the dark." But look how, compared to Dolly, this one is decidedly forward, and like a flooded marsh. She even angles differently. Oscar: cockhound of the Western world, promoting a fool's wisdom. What did he know? Jaffe, with what he felt was peculiar suddenness, was invaded by the memory of the time when he was fourteen and met his brother on the street. Jaffe had had a girl with him. Her name? He pressed himself. No, he couldn't—yes, Sandy. She was a *Sandy*. And later Oscar had asked, with a smirk, "You getting into her pants?" Sandy was thirteen then, and Jaffe was embarrassed that he couldn't give his brother a positive answer. "Not exactly, but I'm. . . ." Her pants? It was an awful moment, one that had stayed with him for years. Getting into her pants? And the look on his brother's face: well, why the hell aren't you? What the hell are you waiting for? Her pants. For weeks he had only been thinking about accidentally brushing a hand over her breasts. Nothing bolder than that. Sandy, his mind lapsed. What happens to the thirteen-year-old Sandys you used to neck wetly with long ago? What becomes of such girls? (Somebody *eventually* gets into their pants, he knew, but he wanted to know more than just that.)

Do girls—afterward like this, lying quietly soft-to-soft —do girls think about other men at the same time, regardless of the one they're connected to at the moment? Or, he wondered, do they think about getting their hair done later, a dress they saw in the window at Bergdorf's?

Her arms were around his back, massaging his neck. His mouth was pressed into a tangle of hair at her ear. He was neither wholly awake nor asleep. Her fingers kneaded the back of his neck firmly, gently, soothingly. Adultery, he thought, sounds sort of like pillory, a terribly wrong Latin legal thing for which they stretch you out on a rack. Why that name? What a terrible sound it has. Come on, it's not adultery. It's still making love, and that's still good, still the same spasmodic contraction . . . the rush of ardor . . . the white meteoric flash . . . the flesh to soft flesh. That isn't changed. So what's with this adultery crap? Shut up and let me enjoy myself.

"You really played the helpless female bit in the park."

"But I *am* helpless."

"You seem different now. More competent."

"Not competent. Com*pat*ible."

"Compatible," Jaffe repeated, snuggling.

"More compatible than I thought at first. I mean, eggs can't tell you everything. I was worried that you might start telling me about love and how you loved me."

"Why did that worry you?" he asked.

"Because I don't trust men."

"What a quaint and old-fashioned viewpoint. It's refreshing to hear a girl say she doesn't trust men. It reflects a certain sense of values."

"You're making fun of me."

"No, just the opposite. It's a compliment."

"I don't trust men and their compliments."

"But I'm not representative of all men. You make me sound like an emissary. I'm me. Just me."

"What's your name, anyway?"

"Hiram Jaffe."

"That sounds like a well-known name. Are you well known?"

"No."

"Are you married?"

"Yes."

"I knew you were. I was testing you. I wanted to see if you'd lie to me."

"Listen, there's something I want to ask *you*."

"Go ahead. Don't be formal."

"Did you make those eggs for me because I was hungry, or because you wanted to test me?"

"A little bit of both. . . . Now I've got a question for you."

"*B'vakasha*."

"What's that mean?"

"That's Hebrew for 'please.' "

"That's what I was going to ask you—if you were Jewish. I thought you were. The most sensitive men are usually Jewish."

"What's with this sensitive stuff? For half my life people have been telling me I'm sensitive."

"So you're Jewish," she said.

"I'm not exactly Jewish anymore. I'm more Zoroastrian.

"Zoroastrian? What do they believe?"

"Well, for one thing, they believe the dead should be buried in a seated position. For another, we Zoroastrians honor God by laughter and pleasure, not by weeping and self-chastisement."

"Do you do that yourself?"

"What?"

"What you just said."

"Well, I'm learning."

"Is your wife also Zoroastrian?"

"No. Jewish."

"What will your children be—if your wife is Jewish and you're Zoroastrian?"

"I plan to raise my children as they'll fit best into the world."

"How's that?"

"As pagans."

"You mean atheists, right?"

"I mean *pagans*."

She giggled, a peal of clear laughter bubbling out at Jaffe, and touching him deeply. He felt a sense of transfer, that some of her freshness radiated right out of her and into him.

"Pagans, pagans, pagans," Jaffe repeated, kissing her about the neck.

"Listen, how do I know you're not kidding me about this Zoroastrian stuff?"

"You can take the word of a Zoroastrian, my little friend. Ur-mazd says the word of a Zoroastrian is sufficient—sufficient and significant."

She returned his kisses with a bite on the shoulder. "You're funny."

"And you're giving me an appetite," Jaffe said. "How about getting me a sandwich. I'm hungry again."

He rolled off her, feeling a wave of relief. He felt that this thing was giving him new strength, and although it might be groundless and unrealistic, there was still a solid sensation of hopefulness that he liked.

Nor did Jaffe, as he lay next to her, find anything dishonest about it, emotionally or intellectually. Plain and simple, he wanted to have them both: wife and mistress. Any dishonesty would be in concealing that. He told her this, and added, "You asked me before what I wanted to do with my life. I can answer you by saying I know what

I *don't* want to do. I *don't* want to lie and contrive. I don't want dishonesty in my sex life or in anything else."

Jaffe also thought how remarkably cool he was about adultery. It must mean, he reflected, that I don't hold marriage sacred. The more he considered it the more he was amazed at how casual he was, how fluent in his treachery.

She wanted to know about his wife, and Jaffe said that he and his wife were estranged. They had recently separated, he said, although he didn't specify that it was a matter of hours, and that by separation he meant he had stayed in bed while Dolly went out for breakfast. The more he told the more he had to exaggerate because he realized that his marriage was relatively stable: some mental cruelty, yes, but no beatings—decent cooking, sporadically good love-making. Probably even a successful marriage. But he told her about being bored with each other, that they were just living in the same house, drifting, directionless, that the mystery had gone out of their love and that it seemed finished. "A lot of people can stay married just like that for their whole lives, but it doesn't seem to make sense." He knew he was exaggerating, misleading her about his marriage, but he wasn't sure where he was overdoing it, because there was some truth in all of it.

"I don't intend to get married again for a while."

"Why?" Jaffe asked.

"I don't think you learn who you are by marrying and having a bunch of kids."

Jaffe thought: how does she manage to hit the nail on

153

the head like that? (Or doesn't she? another voice asked. Is she simply immature and unrealistic?)

"How old are you?"

"Twenty-two," she said.

"I'll bet."

"Nineteen?"

"Is that the truth?"

"Something like that." She shrugged.

He had a vision of confrontation with Dolly, of having to make the explanation suitably reasonable for her. He would want to say, "Dolly, I don't know why this has happened. I don't know how to justify it." And that would be the truth, without lies or connivance, but it wouldn't be good enough. Dolly would cry, as she could do so well, and quickly. Infinitely pathetic in tears. Guilt would strike him and then she'd calm down and say something about love and fulfillment, and give him some clinical stuff. At which point he'd leave. Then, rid of him, her parents would be over the initial shock in record time. ("To tell you the truth, Dolly, we always expected something like this," her mother would say. Her father, for her next marriage, could stand Norfolk Jewry on its head with a $12,000 affair. Look at how happy he could make her parents.)

While he was thinking, she was telling him something about tits and America. "... it's just fatty tissue, and I don't see why men make such a big deal out of them. Did you know that per capita America has fewer nursing mothers than any other country in the world?" (It sounded to Jaffe exactly like something Dolly would say.) "I read in novels that girls get excited by petting. That's non-

154

sense. I remember once in high school I was in a drive-in and this guy was half squeezing my tits off. I could tell he thought it was supposed to make me wild with ecstasy. It didn't, at all, and besides, he was hurting me. Finally I grabbed his balls and gave a good hard squeeze and told him to knock it off. I taught *him* a lesson about tits."

"That really doesn't sound like the same little girl talking."

"What girl?"

"I mean the sweet, helpless thing who came up to me in the park and said, 'Are you handy, sir? Do you know anything about electricity?'"

"I didn't say 'sir.' I never say 'sir.'"

"Okay. So the 'sir' part is exaggeration. But not the other part."

"I was only reversing the old bit. You know—I was the princess who awoke the sleeping prince."

Jaffe turned toward her.

"You woke me up all right."

"Oh," she said, struggling with him, "again?"

"Yes, again."

"Hey look, this is the third time now. Shouldn't you be telling me you love me, or something?"

"I got crumbs in the bed. From the sandwich."

"Oh boy, isn't that an affectionate thing to say."

"Nothing affectionate about crumbs in the sheets."

"Don't be clever. All of a sudden I dislike cleverness."

"But you don't understand. I *am* clever. I live by my wits."

"Then maybe frivolous is the word."

"If it is, then it's a beauty of a word. *Frivolous.* Say it."

"Frivolous."

"It's a beautiful word. Say it slowly. Listen to it roll. Friv-o-lous."

"Will you please stop it? That's just being"—and she laughed—"frivolous."

"I could never be frivolous, and president—even if I didn't have a beard."

"But you don't have a beard."

"I did once. All I ask is that you *assume* I now have a beard. Are you a good *assumer?*"

"Well," she giggled, touching him so that he jumped, "I'm not bad."

He couldn't help but confide in her, and spun the whole story of the mover. In words, in the telling, he had to admit to himself that it sounded strange. Dolly would have interrupted him fifteen times, flinging theories in every direction. But now Jaffe could talk easily, and the girl, a fine listener, smoked down two entire cigarettes while he recounted the details.

After he finished, she lay there, blowing smoke rings. Finally, she said, somewhat suspiciously: "So you have a mover and you've never met him."

"Correct."

"Then how do you know you have a *real* mover and not just someone playing a joke on you?"

"Well, he's got an answering service. And he talks like a mover."

"But you've never laid eyes on him."

156

"No. . . . But my wife met him yesterday."

"Did she?"

"What do you mean? And why did you say it like that?"

"Never mind. I'm just trying to help."

"She said only that he had a red beard, that he smoked a pipe, and that he had plenty of muscles."

"Let's see . . . ," she murmured, blowing smoke rings. "You're sure he intends to move you, from what he says on the phone?"

"Well, that's it. From what he says, he's not so easy to follow. Sometimes you can't tell if he's speaking in earnest or whether he's being ironic."

"So why don't you get another mover?" she asked, crunching out her cigarette.

"On the weekend? It's practically impossible."

"It sounds to me like he's got you trapped. That, or he's some kind of oddball you're attracted to."

"He's odd, all right. At times he appears to be using this whole moving thing as a pretext for playing with me. At other times he goes into long discussions and confides intimate details of his personal life to me, a lot of which seems completely irrelevant, if he's a legitimate mover and all he's supposed to do is move me."

"But maybe it's not so irrelevant. Maybe it really does concern the moving job, somehow."

"That's what I keep thinking. But I just don't see how. You'd have to hear the strange things he says. I'm telling you, it's hard to take him altogether seriously."

"Could he be jealous? Not just sexually, although maybe that's part of it, but jealous of your kind of life?"

"I don't know about that. It's true he's had a different

157

kind of life till recently. A more muscular life. He kept using this peculiar expression, 'making it by muscle.' Now he seems to be branching out more and maybe he feels out of place dealing with people in a sensible way, and doesn't know how to express himself properly."

"All right. Now listen," she said. "I have a suggestion for you. *If...* if you're going to take the mover seriously, then don't take yourself seriously. *But* if you don't want to take the mover seriously, then you'd better take yourself seriously. How's that?"

She swung her legs out of bed and hopped onto the floor.

"That's absolutely Talmudic," Jaffe cried, startled by her thinking.

She bent down to kiss him, and gave him a funny little smile, part mocking, part tender.

"And now," she said, "if you will excuse me, Rabbi, I'm going to the bathroom to unravel my side-curls and say a few prayers. Mind the phone while I'm away from the switchboard."

Jaffe watched her walk away, a lithe, athletic swing, hips flaring and hair tumbling. He had an impulse to leap from the bed and grab her from behind, but decided that would really be taxing himself. She was built so perfectly it was hard to resist the thought.

"Deuteronomy has a lot to say on the subject of feminine hygiene," he called after her. She had closed the door and he didn't know whether she heard him.

The way she looked without her clothes—it was positively heartening. A sliver of white skin ran across her back, around to her chest, branching out just over the tops of her nipples and the underside of her breasts. The outline on her bottom; the white interruption in the orange skin, barely covering her behind, rising in front scarcely an inch over her blonde fur patch. That must have been an amazing bikini she wore this summer, he thought. Jaffe imagined hundreds of men smacking their lips on the beach at the sight of her, while he, who had never seen her in that bathing suit, possessed that firm, blonde, orange body as naturally and easily as could be.

He glanced at his watch. For heaven's sake: a quarter to seven. He'd been here five hours. But what a five hours. He had no desire to go anywhere, to do anything except to lie with his shoulders propped up, one arm under his head, and bask in his conceit. He hadn't felt this pleased with himself in a long time.

The phone rang.

"*Hey!*" He snapped at it, irritated at the intrusion.

"The phone's ringing," he called to her. Water was running in the bathroom and he jumped out of bed and knocked on the door and told her again.

"Answer it, will you? I can't come out right this second," she said.

Jaffe picked it up on the fourth ring.

"Where the hell were you?" the voice snapped at him.

For one bad moment Jaffe thought he was going to faint. He didn't mean to sit down but found himself sitting, nonetheless, his legs suddenly gone weak.

"Wh...?"

"I just came from your place. You weren't there."

"I left you a note," Jaffe said weakly. "In the mailbox."

"I didn't see any note."

159

"But how did you get this number? How... how did you know where to find me?"

The mover chuckled. "It's not such a big neighborhood. There are a lot of snoops who keep track of everybody's business."

"Who? *Who?*"

"Listen, Jaffe, I've met your wife again."

"I don't believe you. You're crazy or something. Where's my wife now?"

"Where's *my* wife?" the mover shot back.

"Oh no you don't."

"About your wife, Jaffe, I want to tell you she's a fine, generous girl."

"What do you mean, *generous?*"

"Generously proportioned. Generous in spirit. Generous all over."

"Why are you saying this?" Jaffe asked.

"She's a southern girl, isn't she? It's true they mature earlier."

"Look, I *know* you're keeping things from me. I'm onto you. You let out part of the truth but you hold back the rest of the truth. You're guilty of mental reservation."

"You're a riot."

Jaffe glanced at the bathroom door. The water had stopped running. What was she doing in there? He wanted her to be here to listen to the way he talked, to get her opinion of whether the mover was mad.

"Let's talk about *your* wife for a second," Jaffe said. "Is it true she can lift an upright?"

"Not an upright. My *first* wife could lift an upright. This one never gets beyond spinets."

160

"And what happened to your first wife?" Jaffe asked. He had a vision of her, blood trickling from her mouth, lying crushed under a piano at the bottom of a staircase.

"Sorry, Jaffe, I'm not going to give you an explanation."

"But you do admit you punch your present wife in the stomach, right?"

"She can take it. She's very solidly built. She used to be a champion surfer in California."

"Well, I wouldn't know about that, but I've talked to her over the phone and she sounds very nice."

"Sounds? *Is*. She *is* nice."

"That's what I meant."

"Are you trying to make trouble?"

"No, I simply mean it's nice to hear someone talk that way about his wife."

"Are you, or are you not trying to make trouble between my wife and me?"

"Me?"

"Yes, you."

"Are you sure you're talking to the right person? This is Hiram Jaffe here." How long can I keep him on the phone? Jaffe wondered. Why doesn't she come back out so she can hear him for herself?

"Life would be hard to endure without her."

"She must be some girl," Jaffe commented.

"You getting wise again?"

"No, I mean that as a compliment. The way you talk about her, I mean, she sounds exceptional."

"She is, but *only* to me."

There must be some way to clear up this whole business, Jaffe thought. It all seems to be branching out, the longer it goes on.

"Hey Jaffe, have you noticed? Something's happened."

"What?"

"Think about it."

Jaffe's only thought was a terrible one: *blackmail.* Was that it?

"You don't see what it is, Jaffe?"

"No."

"You've finally stopped coaxing me about getting you moved."

Inside him, Jaffe thought he heard a groan. He wondered whether it had come out. "Move me—don't move me," he said. "I don't give a shit."

"Jaffe, moving you is no matter of indifference to me."

"That's an odd way to put it, but I can certainly see your point."

"I'm willing to let bygones be bygones."

"BUT WHAT DID I EVER DO TO YOU?" He couldn't contain his exasperation.

"So here's what's happening," the mover said, ignoring Jaffe's outburst. "Let me bring you up to date."

Just then the girl came out of the bathroom, holding a glass of water. She was wearing a white terry cloth bathrobe and she'd rolled her hair up into a bun on top of her head. Jaffe was startled at how different it made her look. He watched as she placed a pill in her mouth, sipped at the water, and swallowed.

"We're having a meeting," the mover said.

"What do you mean, a meeting?" Jaffe signaled her to come over and listen.

"So we can decide."

"Decide what?"

"What do *you* think? Decide if we can move you at all."

"For God's sake, why must I be tormented like this?"

"Jaffe, you don't even know what torment is."

He threw the phone down onto the cradle with such force that it bounced out and clattered to the floor. He picked it up and rammed it down again.

"Hey," she said, "what are you trying to do? Break the phone?"

"That sonuvabitch."

"Why did you hang up like that? I thought you wanted me to listen."

"Well where the hell were you all the time I was talking to him? What the hell were you doing in there so long?"

"Don't yell at me like that. Who do you think you are?"

Jaffe felt his anger receding. "I'm sorry," he said, suddenly ashamed of himself. "It's that mover. He really gets to me."

"You're all upset again," she said.

He nodded.

"Well," she said, sitting down dejectedly on the bed next to him. "I've done what *I* can for you. I've fed you, I've fucked you, I've listened to you. I don't know what else I can do."

"What was that pill you just took?"

"What do *you* think? I belong to the pill-popper brigade. I mean, you didn't care about taking any precautions, and you wouldn't want to hurt me, would you?"

Jaffe smelled a scent that he hadn't noticed before. She must have put it on in the bathroom. Before, she had just had a natural, young, athletic body smell, and now it was so different. And with her hair up, her whole profile was changed, like a different girl. He had a funny feeling in his stomach as he asked her, "Hey, how come you said before you went into the bathroom that I should mind the phone? It's like you knew it was going to ring."

"Oh, c'mon now. That's just an expression. I said I was going to say a few prayers, too. Would you have blamed it on me if Moses walked out of the refrigerator while I was in the bathroom?"

That was just a little bit too fast, Jaffe thought. And she didn't bat an eyelash; nor, for that matter, did she look me in the eye.

Stop it, he told himself, now just stop it. He felt for a dizzy second that he was losing the feeling it was real. Let's not give in to any conspiracy theories. That's paranoid, and it's dangerous—unless, of course, it's true. Jaffe found himself saying his thoughts out loud. "But what does he want? What am I supposed to do?"

"Maybe he wanted you to sleep with me."

Jaffe looked at her suspiciously. Could it be? Is this his way of settling some old score? Of getting even by interfering in my marriage? But how could he do that, unless he sent the girl and prearranged it all? Could they really be a couple of lunatic improvisational actors putting the whole thing on for his benefit?

"Why did you say that?" he asked her calmly.

"Well, maybe I overstated it. What I meant was that if you were here with me, you couldn't very well be at

164

home at the same time. Then he'd come to your house and not find you there and then he wouldn't have to move you—which is what he maybe wants, not to have to move you."

Jaffe nodded. Theoretically, logically, that made sense. But we seem to be dealing more with illogic than logic. And who says he really went to his apartment?

"That could be," he said, "but one thing about your argument troubles me. How did he know your phone number?"

"Beats me. But where there's a will, there's a way."

"What kind of an explanation is that?"

"How about, 'There's more than one way to skin a cat'?"

He nodded.

"Look at that!" she cried. "Look at you. You've got spots of green paint on your chest. I never noticed in the dark." Her eyes searched his body inquisitively. "That really looks neat. You've got them all over. Even *there*." She pointed.

"I know."

"What's the bit? How'd you get them?"

"Never mind."

He sighed, and thought: suddenly I'm in deeper, as though I'm paying now for an afternoon free of worry. "I'd better go." He picked his clothes up off the floor. From out of a dark corner Murphy came over to him. "Oh, hi Murph. I'd forgotten all about you." He chucked her behind the ear and glanced at the girl. She sat looking at him, not responding to Murphy's abrupt appearance. From her expression, she seemed to be thinking.

His shoes tied, Jaffe said, "Well, so long. I'll see you tomorrow."

"Okay, but don't expect a repeat performance of this."

"Why? Why did you say that?"

"It's no good."

"*I* thought it was good."

"*That. That* was good. But the bit between you and me is pointless. We're looking for different things, not for each other. To you, I'm just the girl who happened to be there at the time, and to me you're the guy who happened along at the right time. Get what I mean?"

"Sure, but—"

"No buts. You're the type who'd love me until a better piece of ass came along."

"That's vulgar. You don't have to be vulgar."

"Truth is vulgar."

"But before, you were telling me not to be so serious, and now look how serious *you* are."

She shook her head. "With girls it's different."

"Look, don't play games with me. I've had enough of that lately."

"I'm not playing with you," she said firmly.

"Then I don't understand. Then I don't understand anything. It's like I was born last week and I don't understand *anything*."

"Now don't get melodramatic. Your betrayal of your wife is only...."

"Betrayal? Who said anything about betrayal? I didn't use that word."

She drew her legs up and sat hunched over, hugging her knees. "I've given you everything I can. Everything.

166

But you'll see. When things straighten out for you, you won't want anything to do with me."

Jaffe brushed past her, without a word.

Out on the street, which, in the evening gloom, was still lighter than her apartment, he blinked his eyes and squinted. Within him, a voice asked: will this ever end?

SEVEN

He felt stupid making the admission, even to himself: he had never cheated on Dolly before. It had never been more than an idle thought, like robbing a bank, until this afternoon.

Murphy tugged him out between two parked cars. In making one admission, he couldn't help making another: he hadn't made love to Dolly with that kind of passion since before they were married. It had been five years since Jaffe's last three-times-a-night session. How many times had he made love to her without desire? And sometimes, recently, their lovemaking, at least for him, had been plain boring, once even painful, and several times mechanical, much like two senseless stones banging together.

Dolly's pestering him about making a baby hadn't helped matters any. He didn't know the details of his specific objection, although he knew the indirect objections full well. They conspired in him to produce a kind

168

of fatigue and apathy on the twelfth, thirteenth, and four-teenth nights—the crucial, ovulating nights the doctor had advised Dolly about. But, in answer to her complaints, he had attributed it to sitting up too late and reading, or a night watching television for ridiculous hours on end, while he could feel her eyes watching him, waiting for him, biding time till after he finished the chapter he was reading, or the eleven o'clock news was over, when they would roll out the bed, when he would then complain of red, tired eyes, that he just plain didn't feel like it.

But there were other moments of real desire, sometimes when she looked splendid all dressed up, her dark, short hair shining—that way her behind swung when she wore high heels. Surely that means I still desire her, Jaffe thought. But to what extent—and is it enough?

Yet, what about when she left her underpants dangling from a doorknob, toyed with a forelock as she read a magazine, or picked her nose watching television? Those were things that killed desire. Contempt bred from famili-arity? Maybe that was it. But why couldn't familiarity just as well breed content? So then, perhaps it was bore-dom after all, being bored with knowing everything there was to know about her, and maybe he just needed some-one new, someone fresh, someone for his curiosity, a chal-lenge to his virility. But then, he thought, what would that solve? What if I feel this need for novelty when I'm forty, or every other month till then? Am I made differ-ently? Do I have more universal needs? Who says a man is really made to live with just one woman? Couldn't I just knock off an occasional piece and go on home to Dolly and everything would be all right? Does being unfaithful really matter? Of course it does, he snapped at himself: it's terribly dishonest. But then, he considered, the physical act of infidelity isn't the important thing, is it?

STOP IT! he shouted at himself. STOP LYING. He told himself what he felt must be the truth he was attempting to hide: I'm not made for pure marriage. To love the same woman for ten years, twenty years, thirty years, and never have doubts, never leave her for someone younger, someone different—I might have had grandfathers and ancestors who could do it, but it seems totally unnatural. And who's to vouch for the sex lives of my bearded grandfathers and great-grandfathers?

Who told me to get married so young, anyway? At twenty-four. What was Dolly, the twentieth or twenty-first girl he'd slept with? He had once tabulated it. He had had a theory a long time ago that marriage might free his mind from thinking about dates and getting laid so he could concentrate better on his work. And he had felt he loved Dolly. And for a time it seemed valid: during the first year of his marriage his typewriter's output was good and prolific. Both one-acters were produced.

It's a matter of love, he thought sadly, and it's marriage that destroys love, makes it fade, deteriorate. All that keeping house and laundry and dirty underwear: it takes the mystery out of love. He had a sudden revelation: could it be that marriage is for procreation, not love? But marriage shouldn't be a duty, an obligation. Okay, a voice snapped at him, tell me all this is immature. Go ahead.

He arrived at his building and unhooked Murphy's leash from her collar. It's this goddam move that's done it. I've been uprooted. Something's happening about my environment. Out from a plateau. The next step: Fear. Uncertainty.

"Fuckit," he swore, putting his key in the downstairs lock. Murphy took the steps with her usual vibrating clumsiness. Jaffe plodded up after her. He felt like a trespasser: what the hell am I still *doing* in this goddam building?

Murphy had her nose at the crack of his door, her tail swishing. Jaffe assumed it meant Dolly was at home.

But his fingers holding the key to the lock would not turn. Something was out of place. There was an unfamiliar smell in the corridor. Jaffe sniffed. It seemed stronger at his door, so strong that it lay suspended—dead—more like mustard gas than tobacco smoke. His ear strained at the door. Just barely could he hear Dolly's voice. A laugh: an *intimate* laugh, he thought. And there was another voice somewhere. But was it definitely in there?

Jaffe's face went slack with surprise, as if someone had given him a hard punch in the stomach. For one short, dark, solitary moment, he was aghast. It was impossibly unreal, like something in a dream. But I'm not dreaming. It's incredible. Dolly. Just like that, in there making love to the mover. How could she do this to me? Should I burst in and kill him—or kill myself? What have I ever done to deserve this?

What had he done? What a question. No, a weak voice countered, it couldn't be true. The mover couldn't have arranged Jaffe's affair just so he could strike at his wife. Idiot! Open the door and see if he's really in there with her and not just in your imagination.

Jaffe couldn't. The reality of the scene, if he went in there, would be too much for him. I'm a coward, he thought, slipping Murphy's leash around the bannister and clipping it onto her chain. In a minute or two she'd start to bark and Dolly would come out for her and then she'd know Jaffe had been there. Isn't it strange, he wondered numbly, how minutes ago he had been in possession of two women. Now he had neither. Dolly's voice was inside his head, what she had said to him last week when they were packing boxes: "You seem so preoccupied lately. You never show me any tenderness. You don't ever seem to have time for me. Are you ever jealous of me the way you once were? Does it ever enter your mind?"

He returned to the stairs. Halfway down, he saw, grouped at the bottom of the steps, Gupta, Peter, and Spiegler. What's going on here? Peter? What did Peter have to do with Gupta? The way they were all looking at him. He reached the bottom and they drew back to let him pass, without a word. What the hell *is* this? And then it struck him: they knew. They *knew* about Dolly. Gupta's face looked particularly troubled. It must be that.

"Have you seen Dolly?" Jaffe asked, addressing all three of them.

Each shook his head.

Why didn't they speak? Jaffe wondered. It's like by not using words they think they're not lying. He hadn't the courage to press them. He walked past them to the front door.

"Mr. Jaffe." It was Spiegler.

Jaffe turned.

"I haf somezing for you. Ze moofuh vas here a short vile ago and he left you zis note."

So he wasn't lying. He *had* been there, just as he'd said. Jaffe took the note, which had been folded into eighths. On it was written in pencil:

First man: Do you know what they call movers in England?
Second man: What?
First man: Removal men.

Jaffe turned over the creased piece of paper to see if there was more. There wasn't. He looked at Spiegler, certain he must have read it. From the look on his face he could see Spiegler waiting for Jaffe to say something that would explain the note's meaning.

"Thanks," Jaffe said, stuffing the note into his pocket. He glanced at Peter and Gupta, and then opened the door.

At the mailbox he looked back over his shoulder through the upper glass of the door. The three of them were still together, and Spiegler was talking. Peter nodded seriously. Gupta shook his head. They must be whispering, it seemed to Jaffe; otherwise he would hear them.

He leaned back against the mailboxes, out of sight of the door's window. He squeezed himself against the metal plates, furtively, like a criminal, hiding where no one could hear his thoughts. Jaffe wondered what it would be like to put his fist through that window, feeling the fragments of his deluded conscience collapse like a pane of shattered glass.

The chill of darkness was on the street.

Five minutes later he was back in another doorway, holding a match to the mailbox of name plates.

"You looking for someone?"

He turned to confront a Negro with a garbage can lid.

"That blonde in the first-floor apartment," Jaffe said. "What's her name?"

He had experienced so many small horrors all day that the fact didn't strike the blow it might have. He was only slightly startled by the realization.

"I...I don't know her name."

The Negro was watching him guardedly. "I'm the janitor of this here building and there's no blonde girl in that first-floor apartment." He advanced a step closer to Jaffe.

"She's visiting," Jaffe insisted. "It's her friend's apartment. Her girlfriend's in Europe right now. She told me."

Jaffe wedged past him and went out onto the stoop. He yelled at the window which was behind long bars of steel grating. "Hey, hey! It's me. Hiram Jaffe. I want to talk to you. He took an apple core from the big garbage pail and threw it at the darkened window.

"Cut it out," the janitor said. "You wanna break that window?"

"I'm not going to break it. I just want to talk to her. She was here a few minutes ago."

"And I'm telling you there's no girl living in that apartment."

"How would you know who lives there? I've heard about you. You're never around to fix things in the building when they need fixing."

"You saying I don't know who lives in this apartment?"

"That's right."

174

The janitor laughed.

"Okay," said Jaffe. "Then who lives there? C'mon, tell me."

He was still laughing. "You must be crazy or something, man. You saying I don't know who lives here?"

"C'mon, tell me."

"No, man. Have it your own way. I'm only working here two years every fucking day pulling the fucking garbage out, and mopping the fucking halls. I don't give a shit *who* lives there. Maybe some mother-fucker with a long red beard."

EIGHT

Standing on the subway platform, Jaffe did not want to recognize the predicament he was in. But despite his own resistance, he slowly realized where everything stood.

He thought about what the mover had done to him, and saw that it would be impossible to estimate the damage. Physical harm was one thing, the extent of suffering another. Somehow, he fantasied, he would take revenge on the mover. He hadn't exactly decided how. Perhaps by attaching explosives to the ignition of his van. Or maybe by circulating letters to his clients that the mover was a bad risk, irresponsible, a former bum, drunk, pot-blower, and marriage-wrecker. Exalted by the images, his mind whipped up further fancies. Send him daily notes in the mail, ambiguous, teasing suggestions based on parts of his life that Jaffe now knew about.

But Jaffe realized he could never put such measures into practice. It was beyond his capacities. It was childish. But he could complain to the police. No, not exactly the police. Maybe he'd do best by getting a lawyer to take court action. But on what grounds? Harassment? Or cuckoldry? Which agency could best grasp the significance of the ordeal which he had been put through? It was a slippery thing. What about the phone company? Wasn't there a law against using the phone for the purposes of intimidation? But go and prove it. There hadn't been any bugging or tape-recording. Or was that telephone law limited only to obscene calls? The mover's calls weren't obscene in the normal sense, although they were, in another. But then the mover would say he was only keeping his client posted, and that the client, in the first place, had turned to *him* for services.

He stood there rooted in confusion. He felt downhearted. What the mover was doing to him was so vague and poorly defined. He could come nowhere near, in a way that withstood probing, to making any sense out of his relationship to the mover. And he knew it was almost impossible to explain it to someone in a way that sounded rational. Jaffe felt sure the mover knew this.

The train roared in. He stepped into a half-empty car. It was three stops downtown to his brother's station.

He was about to sit down when for some reason he recalled the famous mad bomber's rampage of several years before, when—among other things—time bombs had exploded under subway seats. All of a sudden, and he didn't know why he chose now to think of it, he was horrified by the thought of a bomb erupting up through his genitals.

Jaffe decided to stand. Sprawled out over two seats next to him a drunk lay cursing and mumbling. Every few moments he would strike a finger in Jaffe's direction, challenging, swearing. Jaffe remained where he was and looked away, pretending not to notice.

All right, Jaffe thought, I'll make a deal. God, he addressed silently, I'll never ask anything else but this: just get me out of these thoughts and get me into that apartment. I'm sorry I ever thought bad things about religion. I apologize, God. I'll be good. Dutiful. I'll try to be better. But don't let me crack up. Show me a little compassion. Just get me moved. *Please.*

Oscar opened the door. He was wearing a scarlet cravat tucked inside a yellow shirt. On the arm of his double-breasted clung Jeanine, his French girlfriend.

"Hello dare, brother," Oscar said.

"Hiram," Jeanine smiled, "where is Dolly?" She pronounced it, Jaffe noticed, as though her name were *Dully.*

"She left me for another man," he said matter-of-factly.

"Glad you could make it, kid," Oscar said, giving him an overly-powerful handshake. "How'd the move go?"

"We haven't moved yet," Jaffe replied tonelessly.

Oscar threw an arm around his brother's shoulder. "It'll straighten out, don't worry. Where's your costume?"

"Under my clothes. Where's yours?"

"Mine?" Oscar said, with what Jaffe felt was exaggerated surprise. "Can't you see? I'm dressed as a fag." He let out a booming, head-thrown-back laugh. Jaffe assumed it was about the tenth time this evening that Oscar had said this. He glanced at Jeanine, smiling lusciously on his brother's arm. There was no question about *her* costume. She wore a yellow silk kimono, with a red sash

178

at the middle and a red flower in her hair. In case anyone missed the idea, she was supposed to be Japanese. She had on inch-long false eyelashes, with the corners of her eyes extended and curled upward another half-inch. It suited her perfectly, Jaffe thought. Her eyes were so big and vacant that a million Chinamen from Hong Kong could have settled there with a fabulous amount of elbow room.

"I will get you a drink," she said. "Scotch is okay, Hiram?"

He nodded, deciding that Jeanine was the kind of dramatic-looking girl who at any moment would be expected to say something out of the ordinary, but never did. She made a gesture like a pouting kiss toward Oscar and waddled off in her white socks and sandals to the bar. Oscar followed her steps and then turned. "What a pair she's got, huh kid? It's funny about French girls. They're usually small and firm-breasted. That's their tradition."

"Tit-wise, you mean?"

"That's right, but not her. She's magnificently big."

"Gee Oscar, you make her tits sound really terrific. Do you think if I asked her nicely, maybe we could go into the bathroom and she'd show me?"

"Wise guy. Always the wise guy."

Jaffe reflected on the fact that Jeanine was the perfect synthesis of his brother's taste in women. Oscar's main rule of thumb seemed to be to avoid Jewish girls. Otherwise, he was an unreserved Francophile and derived real enjoyment from French girls. A surfeit of breasts was also important to him. Jaffe himself believed in what someone

179

had once said: "The bigger the breasts, the lower the I.Q.'s." Watching Jeanine return with the drink, he recalled still another thought with which he agreed: You can lead a whore to culture, but you can't make her think.

He surveyed the room, picking out many of his brother's crowd: David, the queer stockbroker; the *Times* financial writer; Howie, the accountant; Moe Cohn, Oscar's insurance agent. He drifted over to them. Moe was saying, "I sold American Tube at fifteen, and now it's up to thirty-seven." David the stockbroker said smugly, "I told you to hold it, Moe. I distinctly remember that I told you to hold American Tube."

I might have known, Jaffe thought. One of those up-a-point, down-a-point discussions. Rails down, utilities off, wheat and soya beans showing slight gains.

He hung back, watching them. By and large, they were people who knew how to jump in at the right time, make a few points and then get out. Jaffe had heard of so many people who'd struck gold with the market: of shrewd housewives sending their children to college on their successes; barely-literate boors who wore pink sport jackets and drove white convertibles who were able to pile up small fortunes. Was it luck? Was it dishonesty? Jaffe felt that as soon as he put his money in, there'd be a recession and *zoom*, down it would go—a total loss. And even if that didn't happen, he'd have to keep an eye on his money all the time, read the stock tables daily, check in with his broker: shit, that was no way to live, always in fear for your money.

Then he remembered what he comforted himself with: fuck 'em all, it's honorable to be poor.

Look at these guys, the way they can go on and on with their money talk. But then, he knew, there was something in it. The sensation of spending money freely: going into a store and buying a thirty-dollar sweater just like that, or taking a taxi home on the spur of the moment; buying fifty dollars' worth of books on a Brentano's spree; ordering a fifteen-dollar wine with dinner—all in one day. What a beautiful feeling! He remembered the sensation he had had on the day he'd cashed the advance check on *Sing Lulu*. What an expansive, soul-warming, joyful feeling to spend money like that. It must be the thing that drives our society, a part of the human emotions the Communists will never know.

Moe Cohn, dressed as Santa Claus, turned to him. "Hiram!" he exclaimed. "Or is it someone wearing a Hiram Jaffe costume?" His circle of money-talkers all laughed. "Where's Dolly?"

"She ran off with an insurance agent."

Moe wiggled his false white eyebrows and kept laughing. When he had come to his house six months ago to sell him some insurance, he had left his card with a batch of plans and brochures. It said, *Moe Cohn, Underwriter.*

"Hey, Moe," Jaffe felt compelled to say. "You know what I never understood about all that insurance stuff you gave me?"

The Santa Claus face turned serious, helpful and counseling. "No, what?"

"Well, it's this underwriter stuff. I mean, I'm a writer, too. A word-maker, a wordsmith, a wordling, even. A wordelizer. And I know there are copy writers and blurb writers and hack writers. But this underwriter business bothers me. What exactly do you write *under?*"

Jaffe received a thin smile. "Wise guy," Moe said, turning back to the money-talkers.

It was difficult for Jaffe to think of Moe Cohn without laughing. That time at his house, while he was outlining medical plans and death benefits and modest monthly payments for life, Murphy had kept slobbering on Moe Cohn's leg. Of course, Moe had come to the wrong person when he tried selling insurance to Jaffe, but that was Moe Cohn's fault because, after having been put off three times, he persisted in telephoning Jaffe. Oscar was to blame, because he had idly mentioned to Moe that his brother didn't carry any insurance and that he didn't think any insurance agent could sell him. Moe took the challenge. He had tried everything on Jaffe, even philosophy and psychology: "We live in a different world from the romantic one you envision, Hiram. Take my word on that. You've got to carry insurance these days. You owe it to yourself and to Dolly. If you're not covered, I'm going to be worried about you all the time." To which Jaffe had answered: "The myth of security is one of the chief causes of unhappiness in America. People spend money on insurance policies for a type of security that cannot be bought with dollars." The determined Moe Cohn stuck to his guns: "That kind of talk will make a welfare client out of you." Not only had he not been annoyed about Murphy's saliva running down his leg, Jaffe recalled, but Moe Cohn had pretended, in the heat of his pitch, that he hadn't noticed it. Jaffe had felt so bad for him that he very nearly bought some insurance. When Moe left his apart-

182

ment his pants were spotted with drool, from the fly to the cuff.

Moe Cohn's wares also figured prominently at one point in the suicide-prevention-night spent with his brother. Oscar, after the first year of his marriage, had taken out a twenty-thousand-dollar policy, naming his wife as beneficiary. In his depression that night, he confessed to Hiram that he had scarcely a penny to his name, in savings, in stocks, or in the resale value of his decaying, money-eating sports car. "If I sold all my stocks, the car, and all the furniture in this apartment, what would I have—five thousand dollars?" Jaffe had responded, "So what's wrong with that?" "Don't you understand what I mean?" his brother had shouted. "I've got a twenty-grand policy. I'M WORTH MORE DEAD THAN ALIVE."

Jaffe glanced uneasily at Moe. He had an intuitive feeling, a premonition, a kind of reverse *déjà vu:* if they ever had a baby, he'd probably feel he had to take out a policy. And that would hurt. He turned off the thought. It was too painful a step to consider.

A woman in a nurse's uniform was talking with two other women, one quite young, squeezed into a cigarette girl's costume, the other about thirty-five, in a black, floor-length, Mexican dress.

". . . movies and books, yes," said the nurse, "but there are two things I would never recommend to anybody: a psychiatrist and an obstetrician."

"I agree with you completely," said the cigarette girl.

"Speaking of obstetricians," said the woman with the Mexican dress, "I was at Dr. Englander's with Bobby and

183

he got into the *most* fantastic discussion in the waiting room with another little boy, also about four. They were talking about their father's penises. The other kid says to Bobby, "I've seen my father's and it's different than mine." Bobby says, 'How come?' The other kids says, 'His thing's got a mustache on it.'"

"A *mustache!*" the other two chorused in delight.

Jaffe stepped over. "Excuse me, but did you tell him he should say different *from* mine, not different *than?*"

"Oh yes," the Mexican woman said. "You're Oscar's brother. You're a dog-breeder or playwright, or something."

Hiram nodded.

She gave him a dramatic look, sucking in on a cigarette, a theatrical, older-woman-fascinated-with-sensitive-boy look.

"And you have a biblical name—Hiram. King of Tyre. A great admiral."

Again, Jaffe nodded. He noticed that the other two women were making a slow fade-out to the left.

"I have a biblical name, too. . . ."

Jaffe thought it would be indecent to nod again, and so he asked her name.

"Shoshanna Cohn."

"Oh," Jaffe said, "I've heard about you. You're Moe's sister." What he had heard was that she'd won her Cohn name back again when she had divorced her husband last year. She had two kids and a job in the television department of an ad agency. He had heard someone describe Shoshanna Cohn as a very creative time buyer. Men were supposed to respect her business acumen. But from this description he didn't realize she was so overly made-up and hard-looking. "Shush Cohn here," was how they said she answered the phone. Apparently she wasn't about to start Shush Moscowitzing people.

"Where's your wife, Hiram? Moe tells me she's a lovely girl."

"She not here. She ran off with a guy with more muscles than me."

"That's not something to make jokes about."

She had a lazy, nasal way of talking, Jaffe noticed, as though she wanted everyone to know she had said all there was to say, and knew all the answers, but would nonetheless give you a little of her successful career gal's time.

"But I'm not joking."

She gave him a searching look and then confided, "If you have a solid foundation for your marriage you should work at preserving it. Now in my case, my marriage never had a solid foundation. Loneliness brought Stanley Moscowitz and me together. And that wasn't enough. There has to be more."

What's with this wise older-woman crap? She can't be more than five or six years older than I am.

"You should have a dog," Jaffe told her.

"A dog?"

"They're good for loneliness, and once you get past that, you can enjoy them for their own sake."

"But I'm not lonely any more. It was before that I was lonely. Not now. Now I've got a job and two kids."

"All the more reason. Every kid should have a dog."

Jaffe saw from her look that she was unsure whether or

185

not he was joking with her. She was inherently literal-minded but she made a stab at going along with him.

"And what kind of dog do you recommend—male or female?"

"Generally speaking," Jaffe said, "I favor females. They're more perceptive. And they don't fight as much as males. Oh sure, they fight some, but not much. They're not so violent. Every now and then, though, you do run across a really aggressive bitch."

"Really?" she said indifferently, and gave a discreet belch behind her hand.

"Usually, the smaller the bitch the more aggressive she is." Jaffe suddenly found the skin on her exposed shoulders much too white and dry for his taste. He could just see her thighs, all bumpy. "I think I'll go put on my costume," he said.

Having raided his brother's linen closet, Jaffe reappeared with two sheets wound around his body, and a pillow case bound over the top of his head with a black tie. The impression was that of an Arab, which he struggled for five minutes to maintain, but from some angles he looked like a bedraggled, nervous ghost.

"Hiram baby, how are you?"

Jaffe knew the smooth voice: Keith Gardner, account executive. The last time he'd met Keith, also at an Oscar party, he had been the director of a nationwide deodorant campaign. He turned now and saw the false smile, the bristly Guardsman's mustache, the bald head.

"Hi, Keith." Keith was dressed for tennis: racquet in

one hand, a glass in the other. It fitted him just right, Jaffe thought.

"How's the writing game, Hiram? I hear you're getting background material for some new shaggy dog stories. Hear you've got a very interesting little enterprise going there."

Keith Gardner had a polite, self-satisfied voice that treated Jaffe with almost velvet good humor. He always talked to Jaffe as though he were some kind of crank to be humored.

"And I heard you were in the Washington office, Keith."

"Right. We've got a little political account down there."

"You? On a political account?"

"What's so surprising?" Keith took out a comb and ran it through his mustache, twice to the left, twice to the right, and then replaced the comb in his pocket. It was a nervous habit, Jaffe observed.

"But Keith, that's perfect. Politics! You're such a dishonest character as it is."

"Again, Hiram? Again?"

"Sure. Don't you think it's dishonest that in all your TV deodorant ads you never once see an armpit?"

"That's a far cry from dishonesty."

"I gave a lot of thought to your deodorant ads, Keith. You might say they helped enlarge my thinking. It made me think more and more about an America with the conviction to reveal its armpits."

"Ha-*hah*," Keith laughed, patting Jaffe on the shoulder. "Glad I could be of help." He showed him his glass. "Going to get a little refill."

"Hey, you wanna try something terrific? Have some of

187

this avocado brandy. I picked it up in Morocco last year."
Jaffe watched his brother impressing a television director
with a goatee. On his third scotch, Jaffe realized that he
hadn't had dinner and wondered vaguely whether it was
too late to fill up on hors d'oeuvres. He saw the way Oscar
gracefuly turned up the tilted bottle so as not to spill any
drops and remembered what he had said that hysterical
night: "If I wasn't Jewish I could at least be an alcoholic."
He had called himself a sociological case study of the Jew
who didn't like alcohol. He was furious over the fact that
he couldn't stomach booze, particularly since he had to
drink so much of it in company and pretend to like it.
He had cursed his Jewishness and cried that he'd give anything so that he could at least *like* booze. Jaffe himself
often wondered whether the whole liquor thing wasn't an
absolute fraud, that nobody *really* liked the taste of it.

He felt a hand on his shoulder. It belonged to Oscar.

"Hiram, suppose you take it easy on Keith. You can't
just call a guy like that dishonest. Not only is he a big
man in his field, but he's one of *my* friends, not one of
yours."

"But he *is* dishonest."

"No, he isn't, goddamit. And besides, Keith really likes
you. He told me before that as a free-lance you're doing
what he never had the guts to do."

What's with this guts shit? Jaffe asked himself. It takes
so much guts to make yourself sick?

"And Keith liked your one-acters. He thought you had
real talent. He always asks about you when I see him.
You're really much too rough on him."

Jaffe heard his brother out and then took his hand off

his shoulder. "Oscar, I want to tell you something. Not only is he dishonest, but Keith also happens to be a fucken moron."

"Dammit kid, when are you going to grow up?"

"It is not often that I attend parties in the company of Arabs."

The man was dark, about forty, and wore pajamas. His name, Jaffe remembered, was Ben Artzi, or something similar, a manufacturer of Israeli knitwear—his brother's most recently acquired account.

"With imperfect objectivity," Jaffe observed, "I would say that we Americans gave our Cheyenne Indians a bigger screwing than you Israelis gave your Arabs."

"We never screwed our Arabs."

"Save your propaganda for the United Jewish Appeal. I've never heard of an Arab who screwed himself. They're not that kind of people."

"And have you had any experience in Middle Eastern affairs?"

"Not much. But I've had personal experience in the other business."

"I don't follow you. What other business?"

"Getting screwed. I can spot someone getting screwed a mile off."

"And *this* makes you an expert on Israeli-Arab relations?"

"No, it doesn't. In fact, it doesn't even make me an expert on the other business. Sometimes I can't even tell how, or for that matter *why* someone gets screwed."

The Israeli shook his head. "You've got a lot to learn, my boy."

"Will you teach me?" Jaffe asked.

The Israeli gave him a look that showed he questioned Jaffe's sanity.

Jaffe decided not to press him. After all, the man was a client of his brother's, and who was he to take bread out of his brother's mouth?

They were dancing now, bodies circling each other in a drift across the living room, pelvis jerking at pelvis, hips in casual wrestling matches. Christ, Jaffe thought, do these people intend to go on living this way forever?

Behind him, Keith was telling his brother a dirty joke about a man who was walking in the park. He was stopped by a fellow who told him that if he put his ear to this tree he would hear the tree's heartbeat. "So the guy stops and, to humor the nut, he listens, puts his ear to the trunk. 'I don't hear anything,' he says. The other guy says, 'No. Closer. Get closer to the tree. Put your arms around it. Embrace it. Then you'll hear the heartbeat.' So the guy does it, and quick as a wink the other guy snaps a pair of handcuffs on him and while he's wrapped around the tree he steals his wallet and his watch and takes off all his clothes and runs. Well, the guy wrapped around the tree starts to yell and scream, and soon another guy comes along. 'What happened to you?' he asks. So the guy tells him about this other fellow who said the tree had a heartbeat, and how he listened, and how he handcuffed him and robbed him and stole his clothes. The other guy just stands there listening. 'Aren't you going to help me?' The guy shakes his head, smiling, and starts to unzipper his pants. 'Sorry, sweetie,' he says, 'this just isn't your day.'"

His brother and Keith laughed convulsively.

Keith glanced at Jaffe, who was not even smiling.

"Hey, Hiram, did you see your friend?"

"Who's that?"

"The mover guy. We invited him in. He was moving some people down the hall."

Jaffe stared at him, unable to think.

"When he heard your brother's last name, he asked if you were related. Said he knew you—"

"Come on, Keith, how did you—"

"Of course, it's a costume party and it could have been somebody just imitating a mover."

"Keith, this isn't— Why would anyone want to imitate a mover?"

"Probably it gives them a feeling of power. Movers have a lot of power."

"Yes."

"But a mover is hard to imitate. This guy really pulled it off, though, if it was just an act."

Inside his chest Jaffe felt panicky. He turned to his brother who had been listening to the conversation. Jaffe couldn't control the hand that grabbed Oscar's jacket and twisted it. "Oscar, is this true? Was the mover here?"

"The guy with the red beard? Yeah, sure, he was here before. His wife was with him. A real piece."

His heart raced. "What color was her hair?" he cried, as his brother went to the stereo controls, raised his arms, and began making some kind of an announcement. Everybody stopped dancing to listen. He saw a woman smile,

191

Moe Cohn laugh. "What a bit." "Great." Someone said it was a surprise.

Jaffe couldn't hear anything except the commotion in his head: Somehow they found out—Oscar and Keith—and they're doing this to get even with me. Oscar resents my knowing about his crack-up last year. Keith hates me. He tried to slow down his breathing, thinking: It's all a gentle hoax, not a vicious thing. Nobody really means me any harm.

Oscar's kimonoed girlfriend paddled from one dancer to the next, pausing a moment and wiggling, then moving on, charming all, befitting a good hostess. Atop the piano, two girls with long hair were frantically jerking their bodies. The Go-Go dancers wore costumes. One had on a face mask of the Queen of Hearts, the other the Queen of Diamonds. They were dark-haired, wore high heels, black mesh stockings, and the mesh extended up between the two pieces of their tiny bathing suits, crisscrossing in rolling shadows on their waving bellies.

The music was screaming loud. They had been dancing for five minutes in a flurry of arm-waving and stomach-throwing. The others marveled at Oscar's ingenuity. Where had he found them? Jaffe couldn't be sure, but he felt they must be local Puerto Rican girls. The way their hair seemed so jet black. Where *did* his brother get them? he wondered. Oscar had once told him he had to find girls for a visiting client when he was in town, the Vegas account that was always such a headache. Same girls?

Jaffe overheard Shoshanna Cohn saying, "What beautiful figures those girls have. Just lovely." "What do you expect? They're kids. They're probably only eighteen," another woman's voice pointed out.

Shoshanna Cohn put her hands to her ears. "But does it have to be so loud? Where did he get that shouting music?"

"It's one of those up-and-coming rock 'n' roll groups," Jaffe yelled at her over the music. "They call themselves 'Little Freddie and the Cocksuckers.'"

As Shoshanna Cohn took a step away from him, Jaffe edged in for a closer look at the girls. From just under the piano, looking up, he could see that each of them danced in a different style. The Queen of Diamonds was more pell-mell energetic, more abandoned in her hippy gyrations. The Queen of Hearts was more subtle: relatively erect, only her pelvis and hips jerking. Her arms hung down almost straight. The face-mask was red and white and the line for the Queen's mouth was straight and sober.

Slapping her thigh, making her pelvis contract with grab-inward spasms, she looked other-worldly, even a trifle bored with the music's monotony. Jaffe wondered what her expression was like under the mask. He couldn't help but think that the direction of the music, like the irregular pump of her belly, was clearly toward an orgasm, and that she seemed irritated at having to be a party to something so obvious.

Jaffe smiled up at her. Through the slit in her mask, he could see her eyes focusing on him, using him as a point of reference while she undulated, aiming her belly right at the source of his curiosity, which he tried to conceal, by putting his hands in his pockets and puffing the sheet forward.

193

Unexpectedly, the music stopped in a frenzy of shouts. A few people applauded. The girls leaped from the top of the piano, one of them clinging to Jaffe's arm for balance as she landed. The touch of her hand excited him and he turned to follow her.

The Queen of Diamonds came out of the bathroom, the toilet still flushing behind her. Jaffe went in, wondering what had happened to the Queen of Hearts.

Neither the relief he sought, nor the cold water on his face had much effect. He had scarcely eaten all day—just those eggs—and his mind was feeling weary and weak. I must be putting myself through some kind of terrible strain, he thought. He had had six drinks.

He looked up for a moment, as though trying to determine whether he was groaning out loud. He couldn't be sure, but he hoped he wasn't.

She was right at the door as he opened it.

"Well, it's about time. Couldn't you aim for the sides?"

"What?"

"You sounded like some kind of waterfall in there. A regular fire hydrant."

She didn't sound like a Puerto Rican to Jaffe. In fact, he couldn't help thinking, she even sounds a little like—no, that couldn't be. Besides, she's got dark hair. It's because her voice is so muffled under the mask.

"Couldn't you run water in the sink at the same time?"

"Don't you have anything else to do but sneak up and listen to people pee?"

"I know what's the matter with you. Your mother never let you spray the walls with your pee-pee. That's why you make so much noise in there. Like a fascinated three-year-old."

"Are you telling me how to piss?"

"How *not* to piss."

Jaffe reached out to take hold of her, but in a move faster and stronger than his, she shoved him back through the doorway into the bathroom. "Get in there a second. I want to talk to you—alone. You seem like a sensitive kind of guy."

She closed the door behind her, then advanced to the toilet seat where she snapped the rim shut and sat down on it. Jaffe, arms folded, stood leaning against the sink. He was having a great deal of difficulty concentrating, and was aware that he didn't know what to concentrate on.

"Now what's with this party?" she asked. "People keep squeezing me. Everyone who walks past me gives me a little hold here and there."

"What do you want?" Jaffe asked. "An explanation? A discourse? Or shall I just say it must be your costume?"

"Maybe it's *who's* doing the squeezing. These guys are all so creepy. And there are several fags here. I mean, where are the *real* men in this city, men that really work like men? Everybody's married, and if he's not married and he's good-looking, he's a fag."

"I'm not a fag," Jaffe said.

"No, but you're in some kind of trouble."

"But I work like a man, and I'm not bad-looking."

"And you're married."

He looked at the four hearts, each in a corner of her face.

"How did you know that?"

"How did I know that?" she repeated sarcastically. "Take your brother, for example. He comes on like a very big deal, but he's actually a very conservative guy. In fact, he's so conservative he wears pin-striped pajamas."

"How do you know so much about my brother? And how did you know he's my brother?"

"You're alike in many ways," she said.

"But how do you know so much about him?"

The Queen of Hearts pulled her mask forward, bent her head, and lit a cigarette. Jaffe stood looking at the top of her hair and thought she had the blackest, shiniest hair of any girl he'd ever seen.

"Do you think I'm some kind of dunce just because of the kind of work I did in there?"

"No," Jaffe protested. "That's not what I meant."

"Well, that's the way it sounded. That's the trouble with you goddam intellectuals. You're always insulting people. You think everybody's beneath you."

"But I'm not an intellectual. I'm a Zoroastrian."

"Who isn't these days?" she shot back.

Jaffe stared at the way the smoke danced out from under her mask. Was it possible? To stop himself from even thinking the thought, he said, "I'm drawn to Zoroaster, although I confess to a growing interest in Finland. They say that Finns are the most honest people in the world. And that's something to admire. Did you ever hear of an American tourist being taken in Helsinki?"

"All I know is that their tablecloths are damned expensive."

"Well," Jaffe said, "you're young yet. Just don't get into

196

the habit of judging whole nations by their tablecloth industry."

Jaffe could almost feel her giving him a contemptuous look from beneath the mask. He felt it was because he had tried, too obviously, to change the subject. With her eyes on him she flicked the cigarette into the bathtub.

"Hey," he said.

"Hey what?"

"That's my brother's bathtub."

"And it's *my* cigarette."

"Okay, okay."

She extended the little gold-beaded case toward him. "Want one?"

He was going to explain that he usually didn't smoke, but decided to take one and just not say anything. He lit it and felt a surge of new dizziness with the inhale. It must be all the liquor, and not eating, and all that business on my mind. He leaned back more solidly against the sink, wondering if she noticed.

"Ever been in love?" she asked.

"Sure."

"Mind if I give you some advice, based on past experience?"

He could only look at her, half gagging on the cigarette.

"Love someone for what they are, not what they ought to be."

Jaffe nodded.

"Do you think I could fall in love with you?" she asked.

He shrugged.

"Well, I could. I could love you, but it would really be your sensitivity that I'd love, not you."

Why is she doing this? he wondered. Or is it just a question of how suddenly everybody's an expert on love these days? One or two fucks and all of a sudden you're an authority.

"Don't you agree?" she asked.

Jaffe gripped his fingers tightly on the sink, as though asking some silent power to stop her. He felt himself growing steadily more dizzy, and, with the dizziness, hot and damp. He looked beyond the Queen of Hearts to the window. It was open. Why was it so warm? he asked himself.

"Do you—uh—do this kind of work often?" he asked her.

"My friend does it more than I do. She finds it's a good way to meet men."

"Just to meet them?"

"Sometimes the other business, too."

"How do you feel about that? The other business, I mean."

She stood up. "It gets a little idiotic after a while, especially if you've ever watched people do it."

He took a step toward her. Quite noticeably, she moved to the side. "I think I'd better be going out for the next number. I'm only supposed to take a five-minute break."

"First, take off your mask and let me see what you look like." Jaffe could hardly believe the voice had come from him. It was distant and it echoed.

"I'd better go before something disgusting happens."

"C'mon, let's see who you are."

"No, that's part of the bit. I'm not allowed—"

He put his hands on her shoulders and at the same moment she twisted and lunged for the door. But the door

198

opened in, and he pinned her. "There's been too much talk, talk, talk. I just want to get something straight."

"Let go!"

"What was in that cigarette?" Jaffe demanded.

"What the hell do you *think* was in it? Do you think I can put up with this creepy life without a little extra something?"

"But why didn't you tell me? I don't smoke. Why did you pick on me?"

"Let me go. I'm warning you. Let go or I'll scream."

"Talk to me some more about love," Jaffe said, trying to get a hand on her mask. "Talk to me about bathtub love. About water-sporting positions."

"Get your hands off me! I don't want anything from you. I don't want anything from your creepy friends, either. From any man. Just get them to give me my money and I'll get the hell out."

"I think you're a fake. You know who I think you are ... ?" He made a sudden grab for her mask, missed it, and instead gripped her hair. She jerked her head and all her hair came off in his hand, a great black mane of a wig.

The blonde hair piled on top of her head tumbled down.

"It's *you.*"

"You're crazy. HELP!" she wailed.

He had her down on the tile floor, rolling back and forth with her. She was very strong, the way she grappled with his hands. He could feel the power in her legs. For a moment he almost had the mask off, but from his middle he felt a sudden pain where she must have struck him with her knee. He threw his body on top of her, forcing a leg between hers so that she couldn't hurt him again.

Jaffe heard the door fly open with a bang at the same moment hands grabbed him from behind. He was so close, so sure that in the next second he would have her mask off. It wasn't fair.

"Have you gone out of your mind?" It was Oscar's voice. Jaffe winced as he was jerked to his feet. Was it true? Has it happened at last? What difference could appearances make now? Say what you think.

"I accuse you," he said, pointing to Oscar, then to Keith. "I accuse her," he said, pointing at the tile floor where the girl had been.

The wrong one, the Queen of Diamonds, was screaming at him. "Why couldn't you leave her alone. Couldn't you understand?"

Laughing voices broke out behind him. He turned. In the doorway clusters of people were laughing so loudly that he never heard the exact moment when the water was turned on.

The shower was piercingly cold. In the downpour, everything became blurred. He knew they were holding him, and although he tried to keep his eyes open, he knew it was impossible. He felt them dragging him along and fell into a dizzy half-sleep. In his mind he seemed to be nodding, smiling, as if he understood everything perfectly.

NINE

He awoke from a bad dream, thinking, "I forgot to send my parents an anniversary card." Why was he perspiring? He tried to remember. Hadn't there just been something about cheating, taking a math test and trying to see the kid's paper next to him?

A pain from inside his head pressed out. The pressure on his temples seemed to beat in protest as he swung his feet over onto the floor. He glanced at the bed, a couch in his brother's den, and then scraped up his clothes from the floor. He headed toward the kitchen and some tomato juice or coffee. The door to the bedroom was open and he looked in. Jeanine wore a nightgown, and sure enough, like that girl had said, Oscar was sleeping in pin-striped pajamas.

Wasn't it beautiful, he thought enviously, to have an apartment where the furniture was in place, pictures on the wall, the coffee can where it should be. They don't know how lucky they are not to have to live out of boxes.

Christ, if I only had an orderly apartment: everything would settle down. I'd be all right then. And look at how neat the kitchen is. When his brother and his girlfriend woke up, they would come in to a tidy, clean place and have a normal Sunday breakfast. They had had the foresight to clean up from the party before they had gone to sleep. He recalled how just after his brother had met her, he was telling Jaffe about her non-Jewishness and the size of her French breasts and had made a point of the fact that she went around emptying his ashtrays. This had struck Jaffe as curious at the time, but now, this morning, he saw the worth of such a girl.

Jaffe wouldn't dwell on it. He sat, waiting for the coffee to boil, feeling very fragile. He knew without being aware of it consciously that any too deep or disturbing thoughts would have a bad effect. But he also knew that he couldn't sit really still the way he was and keep his balance indefinitely.

It was Dolly that he was trying to keep out: is she still my wife in practice and reality?

How do I justify yesterday? Can I reconcile that blondie without too much fuss? Will I be able to look Dolly straight in the eye? Of course I will; I still look the same. The good part was that it didn't have anything to do with love. It was just lust, and even blondie had wanted it that way. Only a thing for his pride, his virility, his curiosity, with nothing about love binding it and complicating it. That was the nice part, how she had ruptured it and somehow preserved him for Dolly. A disturbing thought crossed his pale, immobile face: oh no you don't

—that dancer last night was just a different blondie, a coincidental blondie.

He felt a tender obligation toward Dolly, to take her out for dinner tonight. He let his mind glide in a way that for him was new and pleasant. It was a little like being saved. Even last night nothing had happened with that girl. It was as if something had kept him from plunging off too far.

I have to stop looking for the body and look instead for the soul, he told himself. I haven't known how to value the sacrifices Dolly was prepared to make for me. Look at how she's worked these last few years. Blondie wouldn't have sacrificed for me like that. She was too cynical. Too flighty.

He sipped at the coffee, and when he wasn't sipping, held his face at the top of the mug, calmed by the hot vapor that caressed his nose and eyes. He saw in the black liquid into which he stared a scene from five years ago in Norfolk, when he had taken a pretty, dark-haired girl to the beach one Sunday. He had kept looking at her eyes, which had seemed to him that day remarkably brown and shining and alive. He and the girl had been lying in the sand facing each other, each propped on an elbow. "I like the way you look at me. Most boys don't look you right in the eye," she'd said. "Why is that?" he'd asked her. "I don't know why. Maybe they catch you looking at them and get embarrassed that you see what they're thinking," Dolly had said. "I'm not embarrassed about what I'm thinking." "I can see that," she'd said. That was so long ago, he thought, and once he married her he'd never thought of it again.

He saw himself standing under a canopy, the Rabbi before him, repeating the words: "Be thou my wife according to the law of Moses and of Israel. I faithfully promise that I will unto thee a true husband be. I will honor and cherish thee. I will protect and support thee, and will provide all that is necessary for thy sustenance. I also take upon myself all such further obligations for thy maintenance as are prescribed. . . ." He hadn't done so well with a few of those, he admitted. He saw the glass at his feet and remembered an interpretation so dignified and poetic that it surprised him; parts of it remained with him. "Breaking this glass also means that in the midst of your happiness you should be aware of the suffering and the crushing of a people, that you, in your happiness, should remember their sorrows and rejoice in your good fortune. The breaking of this glass is a reminder to you, finally, of what love is about. For love, like a fragile glass, can be easily broken. It must be cared for and nurtured, lest by abuse and carelessness it crack irreparably into a hundred fragments." The Rabbi nodded, his foot went down, the glass shattered and splintered. "According to the law of Moses and the state of Virginia, I pronounce you. . . ."

Much later, after the reception, when the aunts and the uncles had all gone, they had sat naked on their bed, tearing open the envelopes, and giggling: twenty-five dollar checks, two fifties, hundred-dollar bonds, two tens and a five. They had stayed up till dawn on their wedding night counting money.

Gupta disclosed his familiar presence from a crack in the doorway, a study in pajamas and toothbrush. Jaffe felt heartened by his appearance. It was so well known, so reassuringly Gupta.

"Guess what, Gupta. I've decided not to move after all. You're right about permanence. This place is fine with me."

"Ih tis a little late for that, Hiram."

Jaffe concentrated not on what Gupta said, but in the way he said, "Ih tis," instead of "It is." He enjoyed that about Gupta. "I think I can work it out," Jaffe said.

He took the steps two at a time. At the door he reached into his pocket for the key, expecting to hear Murphy's excited bark any second.

What the hell is this? The key doesn't fit.

He stepped back away from the door, the old panicky feeling returning, like last night when his brother had said the mover had been at his party. He thought: Spiegler, that dirty bastard—he put a new lock on so I wouldn't be able to get in.

But then he heard the lock turn, and the door swung back. A thin young man in a red bathrobe stood before him. In back of him, where the piano should have been, was an ornate Chinese screen.

"Yes?"

Jaffe felt his finger rise in a small pointing gesture. "All my stuff. . . ."

"Oh, was that yours? They hauled away some of it last night and the rest this morning. We brought our stuff in around nine, just as they were finishing. We've got one room almost set up already."

Jaffe said nothing. His mouth seemed too dry to speak.

For a moment he felt like punching him, but his arms seemed too heavy to move.

"You got any roaches here? My roommate's just *petrified* of them."

He turned and went down the stairs.

Gupta stepped back to let Jaffe in. His entrance was scarcely a walk; he collapsed into the room.

"Gupta, I want to know the truth. Have you seen Dolly?"

"I have only been awake a half hour. In that time I have not seen Dolly."

"Well, where has she been? I haven't seen her in twenty-four hours."

"I think there must be an explanation. If you don't find it presumptuous of me, Hiram, may I suggest that you telephone Dolly. She is probably at your new apartment."

He felt stupid for not thinking of it himself. He dialed the number, and somewhere in the back of his head could hear the number ringing and see Dolly walking to the phone. It stopped ringing. Jaffe's heart jumped.

"Dolly?" he cried.

"Hello?" said a man's voice.

"Who's this?" Jaffe demanded.

"And I might ask the same."

"Oh for Chrissakes, it's *you*," Jaffe said, recognizing the voice and realizing what happened. "Look, the goddam phone company hasn't disconnected the old phone yet. It's ringing where you are and also in my new place down the street. I was able to get my old number transferred. I'm trying to get my wife, so when the phone rings now, just let it go so she can pick it up. They were supposed to disconnect it at five on Saturday, but they had a big mix-up at the phone company over this thing."

"*Well,* I've never heard anything like this. First you don't move out when you're supposed to. Then our apartment isn't painted like it was supposed to be. And now we can't use the phone because you didn't tend to it properly. I've just never heard of anyone bungling a move the way you have."

"WILL YOU BE A LITTLE MORE CHRISTIAN AND STOP BEING SO GODDAM QUEER?"

Jaffe slammed the phone down.

"Hiram, that's not nice," Gupta said seriously.

"He won't let me speak to Dolly."

"He might have, if you hadn't spoken to him like that."

Jaffe took a piece of paper from his shirt pocket and dialed the number on it. Why not get right to the source of it? Call the mover and find out exactly when he took the stuff out, where it is now, whether it's all been moved in already. Let's just find out where things stand this Sunday morning.

The number rang one and a half times and then the operator cut in and asked, "What number are you calling, please?"

He gave her the number.

After scarcely a moment's pause, she said, "I'm sorry. That number has been disconnected."

"What?"

"Disconnected," she repeated.

"How the hell did you know that so fast?"

"Sir, we have lists."

For the second time in less than a minute, he banged the phone down.

Gupta set a cup and saucer on the table next to him. "Here, Hiram, have some tea."

He shook his head. "I don't drink tea for breakfast, Gupta. Especially after I've already had coffee."

"If you drink it, I think you will find it steadies your nerves," Gupta pointed out.

"Gupta, give me a break. I'm trying to think."

You've got nothing of your own in this damn city, Jaffe brooded. Your apartment's not your own. They change the door lock. Your key is made useless. Ah, they permit you to keep the same phone number to let you think they've given you something; but the phone itself is different— beige, while *my* phone is black. They haul away your bed like it was a piece of dead wood. And my wife and dog?

Gupta reached out a long, thin, brown arm and picked up a cup of tea. He sipped at it, then said, "Hiram, we have been friends for two years. Might I say that in all that time I have never seen this side of you?"

Jaffe just stared at him.

"After all, these are just trifles," he went on. "There is no reason to lose one's composure over them. You have plenty to eat and a bed to sleep in at night. You have a beautiful wife. You are a man of culture. You have intelligence and learning. These are the essentials."

"Gupta, I've eaten next to nothing for the last day and a half. I slept on a couch last night. And I think my beautiful wife may have left me. Moreover, I seem to have forgotten everything I ever learned."

"I cannot help but feel you are overstating the matter. Look at it another way. People are trying to help you and yet you take their goodwill so badly. Yesterday, Peter offered to help you move and he was surprised to find you were rude to him. Mr. Spiegler was able to delay the painters from coming in yesterday because your possessions were still in the apartment. That young man upstairs told you exactly when the mover came for your things. Without his information, which he did not have to give you, you would surely find it a mystery. Even the telephone operator told you that the mover's phone number has been disconnected. That may not be to your liking, but she is being helpful by imparting this information to you. Even me. I let you use my telephone. I offer you tea. And then you abuse me, just like the others."

"And my brother's party," Jaffe broke in. "That was a good thing, too, because he invited me so that I could relax and get my mind off the move. Never mind about what happened at the party, right?"

Gupta smiled. "Precisely. Now I think you understand."

Jaffe stood up. "Gupta, some day if you live to be an old, old man, you might be prime minister of your country. And I would worry about that, because I'm afraid that if there was a national catastrophe—a famine or an earthquake—you wouldn't take it seriously enough."

"That is not kind of you, Hiram."

"You have a tendency to justify unpleasant things you can't control by underrating their significance."

"Hiram," Gupta said snappishly, "I am trying to help you. I am trying to comfort you. You are looking for certainty where it does not exist. Judaism has failed you.

Zoroastrianism hasn't given you the answer. Why must you hit it down?"

"Hit what down?"

"The extended hand of friendship."

Jaffe surveyed West End Avenue up and down. He threw a glance eastward, toward Broadway. Is he around here somewhere? His skin prickled at the thought, as if he could feel the mover's presence. He started walking toward his new apartment.

"Good morning, Hiram."

It was the Appletons and their Airedale, Gregory. He gave them a civil nod and a forced smile. For the first time it occurred to him that he was lucky this was all happening on the weekend, when his clients walked their own dogs. Had it been on a weekday, with Jaffe trying to keep his walking schedules in the midst of the chaotic events of the past day, his entire business might have been jeopardized. Who knows? If there is some design to this, maybe the mover didn't realize I stop working on weekends. Maybe he once saw me walking a dog belonging to someone who was away on Saturday, and he assumed that that was a regular occurence. Maybe he is out to destroy me financially as well as spiritually. As it is, he's wrought sufficient internal havoc so that I don't know when I'll ever be able to get myself together and get back to work.

He gave a thought to the play he had been working on, now in its second act. He had sent the copy of the first act to his agent Asch, who had been enthusiastic and encouraging. "Very commercial *and* very funny," Asch had said. But then, Asch had always been enthusiastic and encouraging. Jaffe wasn't as pleased with the unfinished second act as he was with the first. He felt he was straining with it. Maybe it was because he had worked on it in the weeks before the move, and with the smell of the move in his nose, and he had begun getting tangled inside without realizing it.

Now, as he headed south, the problems of the second act seemed so remote as to be part of another world. There were a hundred other matters that he had to get straight first, and each of them seemed more complicated than the problems in the play. He had been trying not to think of the implications of the mover's disconnected phone. Obviously, you don't disconnect your phone service if you're still in business. And obviously, you don't do it if you want someone to be able to reach you. Idly—and unconvincingly —he wondered if perhaps the mover had failed to pay his phone bill and that was why he had no phone all of a sudden. Or could it be that since Jaffe had been his last job before going into his new wrecking and junk business he had closed up one office and opened a more prestigious office somewhere else? But under what name was his new office? And where was his first job?

Jaffe stopped, horrified by the vision: oh no, that can't be it. But look how it fits! What if Jaffe, as the mover's last job before going into the wrecking business had become a kind of scapegoat for him, a symbol of all the lousy people he'd had to move. Suppose he was taking it all out on Jaffe. Or suppose that Jaffe might have become, in the mover's warped mind, his first job in the new business, a special christening-treatment job in which you wreck your client?

"Jeez, you look like the devil. Sumpin' wrong?"

It was his new superintendent, in a clean, pressed uniform of gray Sunday workclothes. Without knowing it, Jaffe had arrived at his new doorway.

"The movers—did they bring my stuff over?"

"Nope."

Jaffe reeled back a step, as though he had been struck. The super's terse answer seemed to confirm his fearful speculations. And, as though once the initial blow had fallen, there was programmed another. His head snapped to the side. A great gunning roar burst from behind him. There was the cry, the blows falling now so hard and quickly, one on top of the other, that he was unable to separate them.

"*Jaf-feeee*," came the call from the truck. As it sped past him, he could see, plain as day, that his piano and sofa were standing in the back of the van.

"Oh my God," Jaffe said in a whisper.

"Jaf-*feeee*."

"Hey, here I am. This is the building. You're going the wrong way," he yelled.

And as he started to chase it down the street toward Riverside Drive, he realized that the mover knew all that, that there was Jaffe, at his building, waiting to be wrecked. As he ran, the thought pounded in his head that the mover had planned it, that he had lain in wait for him, expecting him to appear, so he could disappear like this before his eyes.

As the van reached the corner, an arm went out the driver's window. It wasn't a right-turn signal, but rather an upthrusting finger gesture aimed at the pursuing Jaffe. The arm, Jaffe could see, was big and brawny. It was light, not dark, and it could easily have belonged to a red-headed guy. Jaffe stopped and squinted as the truck turned the corner, trying to see the figure in the cab. The driver was on the far side, and Jaffe couldn't really see with his eyes, only with his mind.

Jaffe glanced to the left, then up and down Riverside Drive, seeking what, he did not know—a police car, his wife, a sign. Then he saw Hobbs, across the street, on the walk near the entrance to the park. He sat like a statue on his horse, surveying his beat, his elbow jutting out and his fist on his hip.

Jaffe was dancing a few feet off the curb, eager to spring across the street. But the traffic was moving along in both directions. He looked north and saw the truck turn-ing off the service road onto Riverside Drive. But would it head north or south? If it headed away from him, he'd be able to see better from across the street on the park side. And he wanted Hobbs to have a look at it while the truck was still in view.

Then he saw Hobbs looking at him. Jaffe jumped up and down, pointing in the direction of the truck. His head whipped back and forth, looking in both directions but not really seeing, and he darted out into the street, heard a screech of tires, and jumped back. He made another false start—five feet out into traffic and instantly backpeddling—then dashed straight for Hobbs across the wide street.

In a second, when he was almost halfway across, he realized his mistake. Before he looked, he knew it was there, bearing down on him. There was no thinking time. He couldn't stop and reverse himself. Out of the corner of his eye he saw the fenders, the headlights, the battered hulk of the cab. The horn was blasting, but there was no squeal of braking tires.

He could feel the vibration under his feet as the truck missed him.

"Hobbs!" Jaffe cried.

The policeman was squinting, looking past Jaffe. Then he was writing something on a pad.

"Hobbs, didn't you see what just happened?"

"I sure did. That truck made an illegal U-turn onto the Drive. I got the bastard's license number."

"That's not all. That's what I came running over here to tell you. He just stole all the furniture out of my apartment. And now he's taking off with it."

"*What?*"

"It's the truth. I swear it. Don't let him get away."

Hobbs deliberated for only a second. "You were right in your advice about the perverts up here. I got two last night. I've decided you're trustworthy. C'mon, climb up in back of me and we'll see where he's going."

Before Jaffe realized it, his foot was in the stirrup and he was swung up to a seat on the horse's behind. He grabbed onto Hobb's middle as the horse leaped forward.

"Did you see the name of the moving company on the truck?" Jaffe cried.

"It was all black. There was nothing written on it."

Jaffe leaned to the left to see past Hobbs and caught sight of the van rounding a curve about three blocks ahead of them. Hobbs must have seen the same thing because Jaffe felt the boots whack into the horse's sides. He swung over to a grassy knoll bordering the walk and urged the horse on.

The horse stumbled, recovered, and broke into a lunging, leather-creaking gallop. Jaffe clung to the straps across Hobbs's chest.

He was scared. What if he fell? He could be smashed under the wheels of a passing car. This isn't what it's all been for, to end this stupid way. He was about to clench his eyes shut, but caught himself, thinking: if I closed my eyes, how do I know where I'd wake up? He was afraid, if it was all a dream, of whose bed he might wake up in. Maybe I'd wake up in another century. Fear of the unknown kept Jaffe's eyes open.

Then the horse slowed down, and at the same moment he heard the barking. It was Murphy, running beside the horse, leaping up at Jaffe's leg, making the horse shy to the left.

"Goddamit, Jaffe, get the dog away!"

"I can't. Not from up here."

Hobbs reined up the horse. "Look, there he goes. He can't do that. He's turning onto the highway. He's not allowed to do that."

"Does that mean he can't get away?"

"I'll call it in right now. There's a call box over there."

"Can I get off now?"

"You can get off and you can hold that goddam dog. Frightened Gwendolyn out of her wits."

"Gwendolyn? Is that your horse's name?"

"I call her Gwen."

Jaffe didn't like riding in the back seat of a police car. Murphy sat next to him, and people along Broadway stared and laughed at the sight of the Saint Bernard with her head hanging out of a police car's back window.

The patrol car had arrived a minute after Hobbs's call. Both policemen in the car, as well as Hobbs, told Jaffe that he had to go to the police station to fill out a form and answer a few questions. At first Jaffe told him he didn't want to go—he didn't like the feeling it gave him in his stomach, even though he felt he had done nothing wrong. But they insisted, telling him that to make certain they apprehend the truck and its driver, they should have maximum information. They used the word maximum three times, Jaffe noticed, and that made him decide that they were probably harmless men. He also felt that what the policemen really wanted was to have his dog in the back of the car. He could see they got a bang out of the way people looked at them with the dog in the back. At a traffic light, Jaffe said to a laughing fat lady crossing the street: "My dog slobbers too much, and they're taking her in." Otherwise, he rode in silence to the twenty-fourth precinct, thinking that he'd never been in a police station before and that he wasn't sure whether this was an auspicious day to pay a visit.

One of the patrol car policemen went into the precinct house with Jaffe and explained to the desk sergeant what had happened. The sergeant nodded and said he knew about the case. "I think it's Sergeant Sawyer's baby. He's handling it in there." He nodded toward a door.

"Wait here," the police car officer told Jaffe, and he went into the room where Sergeant Sawyer was supposed to be handling it.

Murphy looked a little puzzled, and Jaffe told her to sit. When she made a whimper of discomfort, he stroked her head twice. "How did you happen to find me like that?" Jaffe asked her in a whispered voice. "Where did you come from?" Murphy made a licking motion toward Jaffe's face.

"Okay, you can come in," the police car officer said.

Jaffe went into a big room which at first reminded him of a kind of employment agency office, the way it was divided into partitioned cubicles along one wall, with plenty of desks just scattered around the open middle of the room. One man in regular clothes was sitting in his shirtsleeves with his feet up on the desk. Another man, with his tie pulled down and his white shirt collar open, was doing something with his gun. Both wore shoulder holsters whose tight straps cut into their bodies. From the looks of the two men, Jaffe thought, the place could just as well be a gangster's nest.

"Sawyer," the man with his feet up said to Jaffe. He didn't offer him a hand to shake. "Sit down."

The policeman cleaning his gun looked at the dog and called to Sawyer, "Hey George, what's the charge against that guy?"

Sawyer, who was bald, round-faced, and looked like he didn't smile much, nodded at Murphy. "He bite?"

"*She*," Jaffe said.

"She bite?"

"No, she's kind of—" he was going to say cowardly, but instead said "a pacifist." From the look on Sawyer's face, Jaffe knew he had chosen the wrong word. Stupid, he cursed himself, you know cops don't like pacifists.

"How much does she weigh?"

Jaffe noticed that the man asked the question in a peculiarly flat, formal manner, as though it had a bearing on the case.

"Two hundred pounds," Jaffe answered, trying to imitate the serious face.

Sawyer seemed satisfied and looked down at the form on his desk. "Name?"

"Hiram Jaffe."

"Address?"

"Well," he hesitated. "I'm moving today. Do you want my old address or the new one? Because I haven't actually lived at the new address yet."

Sawyer didn't look up. "Address?" he repeated.

Jaffe didn't like the way he did that, but decided to give him the new address.

Sawyer looked at his watch and made a note of the time on the sheet in front of him.

"Did you catch him yet?" Jaffe asked.

Ignoring the question and looking somehow beyond irritation that Jaffe should even ask, Sawyer pointed the point of his pencil at him and said, "Now tell me in your own words what happened."

The suddenness of the question caught Jaffe off guard. He looked for a place to start and almost began, simply, by noting that the truck had sped away from the front of the building where it was supposed to deliver his furniture

218

and boxes of books. He caught himself, realizing that that incident, by itself, was not terribly meaningful. He wanted it seen in context, and thought back and was about to generalize about how unreliable the mover had been, not showing up when he was supposed to. But then, he thought, if they caught him, the mover might say he showed up Saturday evening and Jaffe wasn't there. And if the police asked him to account for that time, what would he say? That he was in bed with a sun-tanned blonde whose name he didn't know? The thought brought on a burst of wetness that threatened to surface any second to his forehead. He decided not to start with how irresponsible the mover was. Maybe he could begin by saying that the mover had been acting suspiciously all along, making ominous, menacing telephone calls. But exactly what parts of that conversation should he recall for them? And they weren't exactly threats. Parts of them were in the nature of a long-winded treatise. Without using much imagination, he could see the look this man Sawyer would give him when he started recalling fragments of those conversations. And he'd have to omit a lot, too. He couldn't tell him about the making-it-by-muscle theory, because the policeman would probably like the idea. How about telling him that the mover had been spying on him, that he knew a lot about his movements, his job, his daily routine? That would seem suspicious. But then, what if the mover just denied it? There was no proof. Shit, Jaffe thought, this is all the surface stuff. He was annoyed that last night he had been idly plotting his revenge and now, faced with the opportunity, he didn't know what to do. If I just stick to the stolen furniture and the speeding truck, then it will sound like that's what this whole affair is really all about. But it isn't. The van with the stuff in it was the least important part. Jaffe couldn't control the snicker he made as he acknowledged the futility, the foolishness of his position.

He saw that Sawyer was watching, waiting for him to say something.

"Excuse me," Jaffe said, "but are you a detective?"

"Yeah." He paused a moment, apparently waiting for more, then asked, "Why?"

Jaffe shrugged his shoulders. "I was just wondering."

Sawyer tapped his pencil.

"I mean you don't wear a uniform," Jaffe said.

"I did—for twelve years."

Jaffe nodded. From the back of the room he heard a commotion, raised voices, and scuffling. He turned in his chair and saw two uniformed policemen struggling with a man. There was a woman, and behind her, a priest. Murphy stood up at the noise and walked the length of her leash.

"Look, I don't have all day."

"Yes, I understand that," Jaffe said. "I know you're trying to be helpful."

"So come on. You look like an intelligent guy. Tell me what happened. Give me a description of the mover."

"I've never seen him."

"Hobbs said he saw him in the truck cab. Said he had a big chest expansion and a red beard."

"That's what he's supposed to look like. That must be him."

"What do you mean *supposed* to look like. Have other people seen him?"

"My wife has. My brother Oscar and Keith Gardner as well. At least they say they did. I'd be interested to know whether they'd say the same thing under a lie detector test."

"Let me understand this. Your wife and brother and some other guy have seen the mover, and the guy's moving your furniture and stuff, and you've never seen him?"

"That's it. Now you've got it."

"Maybe I got it, but something about it seems fishy."

"It *is* a little fishy," Jaffe agreed.

Sawyer tapped the point of his pencil, as though it were a process that usually induced better thinking.

"This is no place for kidding around," he said, a warning sound in his voice.

"I'm not kidding around."

"Then what the hell else are you doing? This here form is still empty. You haven't told me one thing about what happened that I could write down." Then, in a more patient voice, Sawyer said, "Hobbs claims you're a good citizen. He said you gave him some valuable tips. He told me he tore up your ticket."

Jaffe nodded.

"So why can't you tell me what happened?"

"It's not so simple," Jaffe said. "And besides, I don't have to, do I?"

"I should think you'd want to. The guy's got all your stuff in his van. Don't you want it back?"

"I'm beginning to think it'd be a better idea if I didn't

get it back, if I just let him keep the stuff. Then maybe I'd be rid of him."

"Well, what would you like to do? *You* tell *me*."

Jaffe took a breath and sat back in his chair. He had begun to feel a certain relief.

"I'd like to learn Dari, for one thing. That's the secret language of the Zoroastrians."

Sawyer stopped tapping his pencil.

"It's never been written," Jaffe went on. "So no one else can learn it. I've always been intrigued by the thought of a secret language."

"I *meant*," Sawyer said, "what would you like to do about placing charges against this mover that swiped your property?"

"I know that's what you meant. But I was just telling you what I'd like to do in general. About my stuff—" He shrugged. "How much difference does it make?"

Sawyer had lost the formal, bored tone he used in handling routine chores. He looked understandably annoyed at Jaffe's strange lack of cooperation. Also, he sensed there was something that Jaffe didn't want to tell him, and in that, perhaps, was the possibility that the mover hadn't really stolen Jaffe's goods. Why else, his eyes said, wouldn't this guy talk?

"There's such a thing as a bench arrest," he told Jaffe.

Jaffe didn't reply.

"As it is, we're going to pick the guy up for being on the West Side Highway in a commercial vehicle."

"You mean *truck*?"

"Yeah."

"Then why don't you say truck and stop using words

like *commercial vehicle* and *maximum*. That's the whole trouble, not speaking intelligibly. Trouble results when people misunderstand each other. That's what it's all about. People don't understand each other. They talk *at* each other, not *to*."

"Listen, I got my adult education course at the Y for that sort of business. Tuesday nights. There was a guy talking about communicating there."

"That's wonderful," said Jaffe.

Sawyer rapped his pencil against the side of the desk. "So what about your case?"

"Forget it. I'm on the threshold of my new apartment. I'm really almost there. And all this talk is keeping me from it."

Murphy barked. Both Jaffe and Sawyer stood up.

The scuffling that had been going on at the other end of the room was now at the next desk. "George," one of the uniformed policemen called, "this guy says he knows him." He nodded at Jaffe. "I can't make it out, but it's got something to do with that stabbing."

Jaffe saw, to his surprise, that it was Mr. Lopez, his painter.

"You seen this man before?" Sawyer asked.

"Sure. He painted my apartment on Friday. The new apartment. The address I gave you."

The priest stepped forward. "His son, Angel Lopez, was picked up last night. We were all looking for him. Friday night he stabbed a boy who stabbed his brother on the previous day. Last night some other boys took revenge on him."

Mr. Lopez shouted a Spanish curse at Jaffe. Tears fell

from his eyes as the policeman restrained him with a double armlock. Mrs. Lopez was sitting on a chair crying, her body shaking. Her husband continued shouting at Jaffe.

"He says," the priest translated, "that if he had not been working in your apartment, he would have been able to stop the boy."

"It's entirely possible," Jaffe agreed, wondering to himself why the thought wasn't bothering him as he had thought it would. "Is his son seriously hurt? Is he going to die?"

The policeman holding Mr. Lopez said, "He may have some scars on his arms, but they didn't touch his face. He's supposed to be one of the best fighters in the neighborhood. He was fighting two guys at one time when we got there."

Sawyer jerked his head at the policeman, as though waving him off. "It's got nothing to do with my case," he said.

"Nor has it anything to do with me," added Jaffe.

"It's just a coincidence," the priest said.

"That *and* a misunderstanding," Jaffe said. He smiled at the priest. "Say, Father, I'm finding out a lot today. I really am. I wonder if you could tell me one more thing that's always bothered me."

"I will try."

"When they say 'The Wages of Sin is Death,' why is it *is* and not *are*?"

Before the priest could say anything, Sawyer intervened.

"Excuse me, Father, but we're trying to get something cleaned up."

Both Jaffe and the priest silently dismissed each other, without a glance.

"I thought we *were* finished," Jaffe said. "What is there to clean up?"

"That," Sawyer said, pointing to a yellow puddle on the floor next to Murphy.

"*Murphy!*" Jaffe shouted. "*Bad dog.*" He turned to Sawyer. "I'm surprised. She never does that anymore. Especially in a police station." Jaffe took the rag off the desk next to Sawyer's. "It must have happened when she heard all that shouting. She got excited. A female'll do that."

"Hey," said the detective with the unbuttoned collar. "I use that rag to oil my gun."

"I'll buy you another rag," Jaffe said, putting the soiled rag in his back pocket. "I guess I'll be going," he said to Sawyer.

"What are you going to do?" Sawyer asked, as though he feared Jaffe might harm himself in some way.

"I think I'll go home to my new apartment and read from the Avesta."

TEN

"What do you mean letting Murphy run around the streets by herself?"

"She ran away from me in the park. I assumed she must have had your scent."

"She stopped that goddam horse. That horse was going to fall for sure."

Dolly gave Murphy a kiss on the snout. "I'm glad she brought you home safe to me."

"You heard what happened?"

"Hobbs told me. I met him after you left in the patrol car. . . . And your brother called."

"Oh?"

"He wanted to know how you were. He told me you slept over at his place last night, that you had a fight and attacked someone at his party. That you were drunk. . . . He said something else, too."

Jaffe waited.

"He said you attacked a girl and that she was some

kind of a Lesbian and that you must have known that so it wasn't really a sexual thing. He said you seemed to have something against her. He said he wanted me to know that because he said we have a good marriage and he didn't want it harmed by any misunderstanding, something I might hear from a third party."

"That was very thoughtful of Oscar," Jaffe said. "But I really don't believe she was a Lesbian."

"So what was it? What did you have against her?"

"She was being sort of nasty. She had on a mask and I thought it was about time it should come off."

"Then you were drunk?"

"Yes."

"You don't seem so upset anymore."

"I feel calm, in fact."

"That's good. I think you needed that. I'd like to have seen you drunk. Will you get drunk for me sometime?"

He nodded and watched his wife remove a glass from its newspaper wrappings. "What do you think of the paint job?" he asked.

"I love it. It's so bright and animated. I think I'll like it here." Her eyes were shining happy, Jaffe noticed, unreasonably so, considering what had happened.

He sat down on the manuscript-filled suitcase. "I think I'll like it here, too. It's clean, kind of uncluttered-looking."

Dolly said nothing. Murphy stood up and walked out into the next room, her footsteps echoing loudly in the empty apartment.

"Where'd you get the glasses?"

"Oh, I had some time yesterday. I thought the movers

were sort of unreliable. I didn't want them to break this stuff, so I figured I'd bring over some glasses and plates myself. I put the box in the shopping cart."

Jaffe glanced around the room, his eyes pausing here and there, as though taking inventory. "Well, we're not doing so bad. We got a few things."

"Sure," Dolly said brightly.

Jaffe was thinking it was odd that Dolly had said nothing about all her missing clothes, no references to how she'd have to buy a new coat, a whole closetful of shoes and skirts and sweaters. True enough, maybe she thought it would all come flying up special delivery air freight from her father's department store, but it seemed unnatural that a girl wouldn't be lamenting the loss of her clothes. Nor did he see anything like controlled hysterics in her eyes. The bed, the piano, the sofa, the chairs, the lamps, the silverware. She seemed perfectly content to leave the subject unmentioned, and that baffled Jaffe.

Could it be, he wondered, that this is where the mover had miscalculated? Or was there something known by Dolly and the mover that he didn't know about?

"Where were you yesterday afternoon?" he asked.

"I was out looking for you."

"Like just before, with Murphy?"

"Yes."

"But you were gone for so long yesterday. I came back a couple of times and you weren't around."

She stopped taking the glasses out and looked at him. "Do you know?"

"Do I know what?"

"I don't know. It's like you want me to say something."

He glanced around the room, as if looking for a clue.

"Hey, I just thought of something," he said. "Did he steal the box with your diaphragm in it?"

She nodded, sheepishly.

"That bastard."

"It doesn't matter."

"It matters to me," Jaffe said.

"It shouldn't."

"Why not?"

"Because I don't need it—now that you've dragged it out of me."

"I didn't drag anything out. You're telling me something—although God knows what."

"That's where I was yesterday afternoon. You're right. I was gone a long time. But I thought maybe you went out and wanted to be by yourself and you wouldn't notice I was gone."

"So?"

"So I went to the doctor because I'm two weeks late. And then when he told me, I didn't come right back because I thought you wouldn't want it. I didn't want to make you more unsettled. You seemed to have so much more on your mind lately. So I just wandered around most of the afternoon thinking about not telling you for a while. When I came back you weren't here."

Jaffe was trying to recall what he had been doing yesterday afternoon while Dolly was visiting the doctor. Then he remembered, and for a moment went breathless.

His mind plunged over scraps of conversation, different telephones and beds and lunges and grabs, as though all were fragments of a picture that should somehow fall to-

229

gether. "I don't understand how one thing relates to another," he said.

Dolly smiled. "You do *so*. You had biology in college. I saw your notebook in one of those boxes. I'd read you the section on reproduction but we don't have that book anymore."

Jaffe decided not to tell her that this wasn't what he'd meant.

"So," he said abstractly, "we are going to begat, and all our stuff is gone and it's nothing terribly serious, is it? That's where the mover made his mistake."

"What do you mean?"

He shrugged. "Maybe the mover miscalculated. Getting rid of a lot of depressing old junk for me. It was kind of a purge. Don't you feel it?"

Playfully, she shrugged back.

From the expression on his face it looked as if he were trying to do a kind of involved long division in his head.

Jaffe felt he just might have the last laugh on the mover. Here I am back with my wife. Everything's okay. Yesterday's uproar and machinations led nowhere. Unscathed through the loss of my possessions. All the opposite of the mover's intentions. Can dismantling a person ever be a blessing? Swiping a load of his history like cutting something out with a scissors? Wait a minute, he thought, could it be that this is what he really had intended? No, don't ever think that, he told himself, because such benevolence would make even less sense than normal malevolence.

"I'm really dead tired," he said, letting himself slacken in his seat atop the suitcase.

Dolly looked at him, as though waiting for more.

"This father shit is really exhausting."

She came over and sat down next to him.

"There's something else."

"More? You mean there's still more?"

She held something in her hands, and when he opened his to take it from her, she dumped out three bits of soiled, very wrinkled paper.

"What's this?"

"Well, it was a special delivery letter that came for you. Murphy ate most of it. I should have read it but I just got it and then went out to buy some groceries because there was nothing in the refrigerator and I must have just put it down and then Murphy got to it."

Jaffe cupped the three little shreds in his hands.

"This one here," Dolly said, "is from the envelope, and you can see it's postmarked Hollywood." She picked up another piece. "This one looks like the way Asch signs his name, right?"

Jaffe nodded.

"And this one is the really interesting piece. It's got this zero, then a comma, and then three more zeros."

"What's interesting about that?"

"Well, before the zero could come one figure, or maybe even two."

"Maybe it's a telephone number."

"And maybe it isn't. Look at the top over here. Couldn't that be 'call you Monday'—the top half of it anyhow?"

"That's it? Just these pieces are left?"

"Uh-huh."

"Maybe the mover gave Murphy the letter to eat. Maybe

he coated it with dog food so she'd chew it up like that. Keep me guessing."

Dolly poked him in the ribs. "C'mon, admit it. Aren't you excited?"

"I'll tell you what I really am. I'm tired. Look. My eyes are closing by themselves. I need some solid sleep. I think I can sleep now the way I've been needing to sleep."

"You mean you're not upset?"

He put an arm around her. "I don't think so."

"Then here's the rest."

"Now what?"

Dolly handed him a bulging manila envelope from which she took a small calling card.

"What does it say?"

"Read it."

"'Best of luck in your new apartment. *The Mover.*'" Jaffe turned the card over but there was nothing on the other side. From the envelope he removed a big, fluffy doormat that bore the sentiment, *Welcome.* "I'd like to send him a thank you card, but where would I address it?" Jaffe said, thinking, maybe that's a fair swap. Who knows? "A fickle fellow, that one," he added.

For a moment they both looked thoughtfully at the empty, freshly painted apartment around them. Then Dolly said: "The thing is, we don't have a bed."

"I could sleep anywhere."

"How about in the bathtub? We have a great big bathtub here. I could go over to Andrea's and borrow a blanket."

"Whatever you say."

"I think they even have sleeping bags."

"That'll be fine for me, but is sleeping on the floor all right for you?"

"Of course." She seemed to like the suggestion of concern in his voice, and nuzzled his neck.

The phone rang. Jaffe looked at it. This phone rings softer than the old one, he thought. Less jangling. On the second ring he glanced at Dolly, smiling quietly, her eyes lowered. He could see she wasn't going to answer it. She was waiting for him. All right, I'm stronger now. I can handle him. I won't let anything he says bother me. Besides, I can thank him for his present. Jaffe picked it up.

"Hello?"

"Hello?" It wasn't the mover's voice.

"Who's this?"

"Peter. Andrea just told me the good news that you're going to be a father. Congratulations and welcome to the club. I've still got some cigars left."

"Thanks, Peter."

"No kidding, Hiram, that's really swell. I told Gupta and you know what he said? 'Extend to Hiram my felicitations.'"

"That's very nice. You tell Gupta I thank him for his felicitations."

"I'll do that. So long, pops."

"Yeah. 'Bye, Peter."

Looking at Dolly he saw that she hadn't moved during the phone call.

"You know what I'd like?" he said to Dolly.

"What?"

"A hot bath in our new great big bathtub in our new pink-tiled bathroom with the red walls and red ceilings."

233

"Would you like some company?" she said softly.

"Are you going to try any funny stuff?"

"I might."

"Christen the new apartment?"

"Maybe."

"Purification rites?"

"Maybe."

He looked her in the eye and moved his head slightly in the direction of the bathroom.

"I'll go turn the water on," she said. She went out, leaving him alone on the suitcase.

Yes, it was, at heart, a question of ethics. He could hear the mover: where's your sense of right and wrong? All right, he's got my stuff. He'll sell it for junk. Make a profit. Renovated bums need an extra hand.

I can't follow it all the way through—logically—but I feel there's some justice here. It has the feel of justice to it. I know that because inside I don't have any regrets about losing the stuff. I seem to have deserved it. In fact, I even feel good about it. It strikes me the proper way. He went over it again and came to the same conclusion. It must be that I'm not pretending about this. Usually you know it when you're pretending.

A few minutes later he was settling down into the hot water, thinking, how free can I be? How much liberty can I find by disowning all that clutter?

"So what do we have?" he asked her. "A radio, a television set, one suitcase of manuscripts and books, some dishes and plates. A picture of Vishtaspa."

"A rubber plant for our new garden," she added.

"Christ, you can build a civilization on that."

234

She smiled and he took her hand as she stepped into the water.

"We can build around that, can't we?"

"I don't see why not," she said.

"A fresh start."

"Right."

Is this it? he wondered. Can the whole thing just end this way? Sure. Why not? Without wanting to spare himself, Jaffe admitted that it was possible he would never know the details of what had happened to him this weekend or the reasons why it had happened. He felt somehow confirmed in his uncertainties, and that seemed enough.

"The water's hot," she said.

"Very hot."

She sat down facing him and smiled.

"Biggest bathtub I've ever been in," said Jaffe.

She continued smiling, beaming actually.

"It's the old-fashioned kind. Did you see the legs?"

She shook her head and her loose hair swung back and forth.

He slid over close to her and bent his head forward. She began pouring the water on him, the hot, foamy wetness meeting within him a soft call that he had nearly forgotten existed. His turmoil seemed so diminished, a thing past, and he said to her, "I'm glad we didn't stay in that other apartment," thinking to himself of a place where exhausted old piano teachers lived out their last days on the top floor.

As the water streamed down his neck and shoulders, his confidence became something radical. He felt possessed, as if he could do anything, no matter how enormous or trivial: translate the Book of Zoroaster into Sanskrit or carve a meerschaum, anything he set his mind to.

Then she stopped and he turned around and she moved sideways and hung her head. He cupped his hands and scooped at the water, spilling it over her. He thought it was interesting how they were treating each other with great gentleness, as if they were both invalids.

"Hey Dolly, we don't have any towels."

"Ssshh."